MW01490171

Cold Spring

GLENN SHAPIRO

PALMETTO
PUBLISHING
Charleston, SC
www.PalmettoPublishing.com

Hardcover ISBN: 9798822959644
Paperback ISBN: 9798822959651
eBook ISBN: 9798822959668

For Nancy

Prologue

The sky looked to be in mid-decision between light and darkness, when the first and brightest of stars begin to faintly appear, but the treetops are not yet fully silhouetted and reveal some features to the naked eye. Cole lay on the firm ground of his campsite and Belinda leaned over him whispering something almost inaudibly. With the rapidly fading light behind her, he could barely make out her features, but he could see her eyes, blue and clear. Her eyes always struck him, even in passing glances. They were blue with a tight black outline around the iris that made them appear almost crystalline in the center. It's why he affectionately called her Blue.

Her face came into sharper view, lit from some unseen source, and her voice now rang clear, almost echoing as she said, "Cole. Come home."

Cole sprang awake with a jerk to his head and chest. He was momentarily in the confused fog between sleep and consciousness, but the crisp night air roused him to his senses. His mind went back to his dream. He almost never remembered his dreams, but this was so vivid it felt more like a memory than a dream and took on immediate meaning to him. Cole Thomas was raised in a Christian family, but the full faith had never really taken hold of him. However, he had a deep sense that there were guiding forces and meaning in the events that surrounded everyday life. This particular moment was rich with that feeling. His small campsite was deadly quiet. The last embers of a fire gave off the faintest of glows, so slight as to seem like he was imagining the light. The air was cool and motionless, and stars speckled the sky. His senses were keenly alert and yet focused on things beyond the sound, smell, or feel of the moment. He was deciding whether he had truly been called home. Everything in him and around him told him he had.

April 1844 – Hudson Valley, New York

Cole awoke to the usual chorus of birds surrounding the Thomas farmhouse early on an April morning. He felt the familiar crisp air of New York's Hudson Valley blowing in through the open window. The two-bedroom farmhouse was whitewashed on the outside, with a small, raised front porch and four steps to the ground. It sat amid a fifteen-acre family farm with fertile land in which the Thomas's grew a rotation of corn, wheat, and rye. Furnishings were sparse. There was nothing, beyond their mattresses in the bedrooms, and the family area had a rocking chair and a small table with three rough-looking wooden stools, all made by his grandfather. There were no curtains and no art or other adornments on the walls. Ma would say that she never saw the point in such frivolities.

The only other structure on the farm was a barn where two milking cows, a plow horse, and a cart horse were kept overnight. They grazed in a small pasture that used about three of their fifteen acres. The house and barn sat on a plot of about an acre with grass and a large vegetable garden that supplied the family with green beans, tomatoes, beets, and potatoes. Rhubarb stalks sprouted at the edge of the garden and supplied the family with their most cherished treat, Ma's rhubarb pie.

Ma was up, and Cole heard the familiar sounds of bustling in the kitchen as she prepared breakfast. Cole was typically the second to rise but sometimes he was up before his mom, which gave him a sense of pride on those days. Elizabeth Thomas was a force, the rare woman who had lost her husband but had no interest in seeking out a new one. Most folks felt that a new man in the house before the next winter was the only path to survival. They had now passed two winters since her husband had gone. Cole rolled off his hay-stuffed mattress, made of several flour sacks stitched together, and stepped over his older brother, Dale, who seemed to be able to sleep regardless of what stirred around him.

Dale was six years older and already looked like a man at seventeen. He had a thick reddish-brown beard and wide shoulders. He even had the start of a belly as would be seen on a man of thirty. His squat nose gave him a somewhat pug look. He didn't smile that often but was amiable enough. Ma would tell Cole that his brother loved them both, but he was just a quiet, serious sort.

Cole, at age eleven, was short and skinny but wiry and strong. Some of the boys, and girls, his age were a head taller and twice his weight. Despite their size difference, he could do most of the work equal to Dale, from lifting hay bales to pulling out saplings in the outer fields. Cole had thick eyebrows and dark eyes, almost black, that shined. Shoulder-length brown hair surrounded his narrow face, which almost always bore a smile, the kind that made many people wonder what he was up to.

The smell of eggs and bacon caught Cole's nostrils and he quickly went to the table and pulled out a stool. Ma said, "You wash up before food. We aren't animals."

"Yes, my lady." Cole gave a deep, facetious bow and flashed his usual impish smile to his mother, which brought an eye roll and the faintest hint of a grin back from her.

Elizabeth Thomas was thirty-nine but looked older. Her brown hair had grayed around the temples and thinned a bit. Her skin was weathered, as was the case with most farmers. She was fit and strong. She weighed no more than one hundred ten pounds but could heft that much weight or more when needed. Her light brown eyes were deep set and could be piercing or loving with equal intensity.

"Today you and your brother will start weeding the wheat in the back field. We'll need that full field cleared of weeds by the end of the week, while you're off from school, so you'd best plan out the time to get it done. Take advantage of the good weather today in case it rains later in the week."

"I hate weeding." Cole dropped his forehead on the table dramatically.

"Well, they won't pull themselves, and I'm starting in the front fields to ready them for plowing and planting the corn next month."

The eleven cultivated acres on their family farm consisted of a crop rotation between corn, wheat, and rye. This year they would have corn and wheat only, with corn taking up the larger front fields, which totaled eight acres, and wheat in the three-acre back field. Wheat sold for more money but took more labor to farm.

Ma placed three fried eggs and two thick cuts of bacon on his wooden plate and Cole ate it all in moments. Cole did everything fast. He ate fast, walked fast, and completed his chores fast. He even thought fast. He could compute sums quicker than any of his friends and would come up with answers at school so quickly that classmates would groan in frustration.

As Ma left to drag Dale from bed, Cole jumped up and cut a small piece of bacon from an end where he hoped it would not be noticed and then stuffed it in his pocket. A few moments later, with a great deal of moaning and protestation, Dale emerged. He thumped down hard on a stool and rested his head in his hands as if to return to his slumber at the table. But when the bacon and eggs arrived, the allure was strong enough to rouse him.

Cole looked over at his older brother, with his beard still flat on one side from sleep, and said, with feigned excitement, "We get to weed the back field today, and all this week, Dale."

Dale just grunted, which was as much as he usually said.

Cole turned to Ma. "The new folks took over the Leary farm last week. Can I go have a look while we are out in the back field? Word is they've got four kids from Dale's age down to younger than me."

"Leave them people alone unless we get an invitation. They'll have their work cut out for them, as that place's been untended for more than a year now. And the damned place is cursed anyhow." Her expression turned dark, and she looked out the window across the fields. Meg Leary had been Ma's closest friend and had been gone for more than a year.

"But Ma ..." Cole began to protest. Ma just walked from the room.

Dale finally spoke and said "Dumbass. You know she can't think about that place."

"Why? I know those poor kids died of scarlet fever and the Leary's left town. But she may see Miss Meg again someday."

Dale became hushed and thoughtful. His eyes darted to the other room, ensuring he was not heard, and his brow furrowed deeply as he strained to decide what to say or whether to say it. "They didn't leave town, Cole. Ma, and lots of other folks, just told their kids that. They killed themselves with a shotgun in the barn after their last one, Sissy, passed. Ma found them when she was bringing a stew over. Now don't say nothin' about this cuz you're not supposed to know. Just don't talk about that place to Ma."

Cole was stunned into silence and gave Ma a long hug before leaving for his chores.

...

Cole and Dale walked to the back fields. The day was perfect for weeding. The sky was a clear blue. A slight breeze blew across the fields and cooled an already crisp day. You could work in this temperature and not even break a sweat.

They walked a central path between the two four-acre front fields that would be planted with corn in May. Now, they lay bare with deep brown, almost black, soil that promised a healthy crop.

The back fields bent just enough downhill that the farmhouse sank into the fields behind them until only the weathervane rose above the horizon and then was lost a few steps later. The wheat bent gently in the breeze and shone like gold in the low morning sun. The sound of the soft wind through the wheat layered above the babble of the river just down the hill. Cole reflected that these were the days when their farm felt like heaven.

Ahead of them, the border between their farm and the Leary land was marked by a patch of trees and a crude fence that was no more than tree limbs pounded into the earth and wrapped with wire that encircled each post and then stretched to the next. Three fence wires ran parallel to the ground about eighteen inches apart. Easy for the boys to step through but enough to keep any livestock on their own side.

At the fence line, Cole saw movement. Ducking under the lowest wire was a stray dog that had become a staple of their morning routine on the farm. Cole beamed and shouted out, "Hey boy. I've got your breakfast." The dog ran with enthusiasm, his ears flopping up and down with each stride as if he were trying to take flight. As he reached the boys, Cole removed the cut of bacon from his pocket and fed the hungry dog, who gobbled it down in seconds.

"You know if you keep feeding him, he won't stop coming here," Dale grumbled in his usual monotone.

"Exactly," said Cole, smiling and scratching behind the dog's dirty ears.

The dog was gray with medium-length, shaggy, dirty fur. His back stood just above Cole's knee as he leaned against him. His face was narrow, and he had wiry wisps of a beard. His underbite revealed his lower teeth, with his left lower fang missing, which made the right one stand out. Despite being scraggly, dirty, and missing that tooth, he seemed young, perhaps no more than a year old. His alert eyes shone with excitement at the attention he was getting.

"I'm going to ask Ma if we can keep him. I'm going to call him Tusk."

Dale just shook his head. "Well, let's get to work."

Cole nodded in agreement and said, "Dale, we've got three acres to weed and six days to do it. That's a half-acre a day between us or about ten thousand square feet for each of us each day. If we think about it like ten-by-ten squares, we each need to do one hundred in a day." Cole paused to think briefly. "And that means about five minutes for each square for eight hours. Give or take. Would be good to get ahead of that today with the good weather."

Dale started to do the math and then decided not to bother. He knew his brother was a whiz with figures and always did them right. They started in the southwest corner, each estimating a ten-by-ten square and clearing it of weeds, then shifting to the next ten-foot swath to the north, working in side-by-side rows. It soon became like a slow-running race of who could advance farther.

...

At noon they decided to walk back for their midday meal. Cole glanced out at the work done so far, more than a quarter acre weeded. "We're on a good pace," he said to his brother. Then he saw movement in the trees just beyond the fence. Tusk was lying near the boys, likely hoping there was more bacon to be had. "Hey, Dale, there's someone in the trees on the Leary side over there."

Dale looked. "Maybe one of the new kids."

There was no more movement, and they turned for home. Tusk followed, which was the first time he had done that. Cole mused as to whether the dog had understood his intention to ask Ma to keep him. He always felt that things happened for a reason, and now this dog seemed less like a chance meeting and more like a soul bound to him.

Arriving home, Dale opened the screen door leading from the front porch inside. Cole followed, and to his surprise, Tusk walked in next to him. Ma appeared and pointed. "What is that animal doing in my house?"

Cole was dumbfounded and managed no more than a stuttering "Uh." Dale put his hands up, his way of saying, "This has nothing to do with me."

Ma stared at the dog, who cocked his head to one side and stared back. No one said a word for at least a minute. Finally, she said, "Well, he's your responsibility, not mine. And after planting today, you're going to wash him up, so he doesn't stink."

Stunned and at a loss for words, Cole just dropped to his knees and threw his arms around Tusk, his dog, who seemed to look pleased with himself.

...

The brothers worked until sundown and finished up for the day. They were satisfied with a good day's work and a lot of progress, with nearly three-fourths of an acre weeded. They worked well together, though there was little conversation. The few words spoken were from Cole, and Dale would nod and give the occasional "yup." Cole appreciated Dale though because he was unlike other big brothers. His friends at school would talk of getting picked on, yelled at, and occasionally beat up by their bullying older brothers. Dale rarely had a harsh word, or any words for that matter, and had never hit Cole.

As they wrapped up their work, picked up their tools, and prepared to head back to the farmhouse, Cole said, "I'm going to take a look by the fence into the Leary land."

"You heard Ma," Dale warned.

"I know, but I am only going to look. I'll see you at home."

Dale shrugged and turned toward home. Tusk had been lying nearby, apparently not willing to let his new owner out of his sight. Seeing the shift in action, he trotted over and took his place by Cole's side. The two walked toward the fence.

As they approached the fence, shaded by the trees at the border, Tusk took off and bounded through the wires and into the tree line. Cole called after him and then wondered how long it took a dog to know his name. As he arrived at the fence, he heard rustling and saw movement. "Who's there?"

No answer came and he stepped cautiously through the horizontal wires on the boundary. Peering through the underbrush, he could see Tusk's tail wagging, so he took a step in and pushed aside some lower foliage. Tusk stood in front of a girl Cole guessed was about his own age, sitting on the ground.

"Hello?" Cole said, but it came out like a question.

"Hi," the girl responded while glancing up quickly and then returning her gaze to Tusk.

"Do you like my dog?" Cole asked.

"Your dog? I didn't know he had an owner. I've been feeding him since we moved in."

Cole smiled. "I guess he gets food wherever he can. I suppose he's only been my dog for a few hours anyway."

She looked at him puzzled.

"I just asked my mom, and … Anyway, I suppose you moved into the Leary house."

"Yeah." She stood and took a step forward. Cole could see her more clearly now. Her eyes were the first thing he saw, the brightest blue he'd ever seen. She was about his height and about as skinny. Her hair was a dirty blonde at the top but lightened in sun-bleached strands as it fell down to her shoulders. She wore a dirty sundress, and a sea of freckles showed on her face, neck, and arms. There was a bruise on her cheek that looked fresh.

She was studying him closely. Her bright blue eyes narrowed as she examined his face. "Your hair's as long as mine," she said in an appraising way as she leaned even closer. "And your eyes are so dark. They're like pieces of coal."

Cole smiled and said, "Well I guess that works cuz that's my name. Cole."

She laughed and said, "I'm Belinda."

Cole thought and stared at the girl he'd just met. For the

second time today, he felt that things had happened for a reason. Tusk was brought to him, and Tusk brought him here. A wry smile crept onto his face, and he said, "Well I suppose if I'm Cole, like my eyes, I'll call you Blue."

...

The rest of that week followed the same routine. The boys woke up each morning and ate the breakfast Ma prepared before heading to the back wheat field to weed. The freshly washed Tusk was even allowed to sleep in the boys' room. Ma would gather up scraps and bits of fat from the bacon after breakfast and gruffly say she'd rather give it to the dog than just throw it out, but neither boy believed her. She was soft for Tusk already.

Each day they made great progress on the wheat fields while Tusk waited close by, and each late afternoon, Tusk would run through the fence to Belinda and Cole would follow. On the last day of weeding, they finished by midafternoon. Cole ran to meet his new friend, hardly able to wait to see her. He'd realized she wasn't like any girl he had known. The girls at school kept to their own group and didn't like the boys, or at least pretended not to. They worried about their hair or dresses and talked gossip.

Blue liked to talk about dreams for the future, what made plants grow, or where animals came from. She liked to play in the dirt and run. Her knees were always dirty and scabbed. Cole thought to himself, *she's kinda like a boy*, though he never said that to her.

He'd learned that Belinda was one of four kids in the Wright family. Tommy was a year older than Dale; Belinda was next at eleven years old, and there were two little ones; five-year-old Alice and three-year-old Buck. She hadn't talked much about her mom and dad, and something made Cole not ask.

Today he found Belinda, and she was hugging Tusk tightly. The scruffy dog buried his head in the crook of her neck in what appeared to be his way of hugging back. When she looked up, the first thing he saw was the color of her eyes, as always. They were not just brilliant blue today; they were wet and somehow even more brilliant than usual. The second thing he noticed was a split lower lip. She held a rag in her hand that was splotched with blood.

"What happened?" Cole said softly, almost in a whisper.

Belinda hesitated, looking at the rag in her hand, then asked, "Can you keep a secret?"

"Of course. Cross my heart."

"Tommy happened."

"Your brother? Why … I mean … you're his sister?"

She looked down, "I guess you'd have to ask him. He's been like this for a while. He wasn't always—he loved me when I was little. For some reason, he got angry with me, and he's never said why."

"Don't your parents stop him? I mean, doesn't he get whooped?"

Belinda looked down and shook her head. She said softly, "You need to go home now, please." Her emphasis was on *please*.

Cole stood, looking at his friend. He had never seen such sadness in a person as he saw in that moment. It made him realize in a flash that he had lived a sheltered and blessed life.

He wanted to hold her hand and tell her it would be OK. He wanted to refuse her plea and stand with his friend. But he just nodded and turned toward home. As he reached the fence, he looked back and saw Belinda dig a small hole and bury the bloody rag. Then she got up and ran home. Tusk went with her.

...

Sunday morning after breakfast, Ma, Dale, and Cole began their routine for church. Cole washed his hair and face in the tin basin full of cold well water. In winter Ma would heat a pot of water and mix it in to make it bearable, but at this time of year, they washed in cold water. He put on his brown corduroy pants and his only white cotton shirt. It had black buttons and a pocket sewn into the left breast. He tucked his long, wet hair behind his ears and presented himself to Ma. She put on an intentionally furrowed brow to convey a serious inspection and declared her verdict. "Very handsome."

Dale washed up and emerged for his inspection. He still had a little soap in his beard and had misaligned the buttons on his shirt so that the left bottom hung lower than the right. Dale didn't care much about his appearance. Ma wiped his beard and quickly refastened his buttons without a word and then proclaimed again, "Very handsome."

Ma dressed plainly in a gray, shapeless frock. Like her house, she saw little need to adorn herself. To do so would have been frivolous. But she did like her boys to look nice. They were her reflection on the world.

They arrived at the small church that seated less than fifty people and was typically just over half full. Everyone knew everyone else. Before mass, there was a round of greetings with men talking of the crop or hunting, while ladies caught up on what was happening around town.

There was a noticeable hush as the new family walked in the front door. Cole turned to look and saw Belinda and her family. His eyes landed on her first but as he scanned the family around her, he realized he had asked her a dumb question in her moment of pain.

Belinda's mother was a short, frail-looking woman with black, gray-streaked hair. Her face was pleasant, and you could imagine her as having been attractive at one time, but she seemed to shrink as she walked up the aisle. Her shoulders slumped and she held her hands together in front of her chest, as if praying not to be seen. Belinda's father was only slightly larger than his wife and held a vacant expression. He looked as if he had stumbled out of a bar moments before mass. His reddish hair was uncombed, and his clothes were disheveled. His walk gave away that he had been at the bottle. Cole had seen enough men in that state to recognize it.

Behind the parents, the hulking figure of Tommy was a stark contrast. He was tall and broad. He walked with his shoulders back and cast around the church with a confident stare for anyone who met his eye. He had dark, straight hair, just covering his ears. His square jaw jutted forward at his chin and his eyes were dark below thick black brows. Cole was staring at him, and their eyes met. Cole wanted his stare to say, "I know what you did," or, "Don't you dare hurt my friend," but instead, he broke the stare immediately and looked away, feeling ashamed and weak. It was obvious in just seconds of observation that Tommy could do what he wanted, and his parents were not going to intervene.

The two little ones bounced in after with the joyful oblivion of young children. Alice looked like what Cole could imagine Belinda being at age five. Buck was fair-skinned and looked small, even for three years old.

Cole looked at Belinda, hoping she would look up at him, but she seemed aware and avoided his gaze. He thought to himself that a brave man would go talk to her or even challenge Tommy for what he had done. The procession was starting, and Cole just sat down.

July 1846 – Cold Spring, New York

Cole and Belinda spent every spare moment together, after school, after chores, they even snuck out their windows at night sometimes and lay in the fields between their homes, staring up through wheat or rye at the stars. There seemed to be no end to what they could talk about or the time they could spend together, even without talking.

Of course, they were not often alone because Tusk would tag along, rarely leaving one or the other's side. Cole would laugh and say, "Tusk is *our* dog." It was a joke, but it also made him feel good. It gave permanence to their friendship and made him feel more grown up.

The two of them had grown at about the same pace and remained skinny, wiry frames with hair to their shoulders. They had been mistaken for siblings more than once.

Every week or two, Blue would have some new injury at the hands of her brother. Each time, Cole would resolve to do something about it. To be brave. But each time, the two of them would ignore the injury and move on to whatever adventure they planned for the day.

It was a Saturday in July and it had been scalding hot all week. Having completed their chores, and being on summer vacation from school, Cole and Blue were walking into town.

There had been a general town center for several years; a collection of small shops for supplies. Just this year though, they had officially become a town, Cold Spring, New York. It gave all of the locals a new sense of pride and belonging to have an official town charter.

As they walked along the winding dirt road that ran two miles to town from the collection of family farms that included their own, they played a game of kicking rocks and trying to get them past each other's legs. Tusk hung back to stay clear of the flying rocks.

Just outside of town, an older man was on the opposite side of the road, carrying a sack over his shoulder. They didn't recognize him, and he barely looked up, when he said, "Good morning, boys."

Cole nodded and waved and when he was around the corner fell over with laughter. "D'you hear that? He thought we were both boys. What do ya say to that, Blue, fella?"

Belinda crossed her arms and scrunched her face but made no reply to that. She simply said, "Are we going into town or not?"

The general store had freshly made ice cream on Saturdays and that is what they had journeyed for. Pulling a coin that Ma had given him as his monthly allowance, Cole eagerly ordered two ice creams and they sat on the stoop of the store eating it down in the hot sun. As they stood to leave the stoop, a woman approached the store steps and Cole grabbed the door to hold it for her, with Belinda by his side. The woman was busy with her purse as she walked in but did turn to say, "Why, thank you, girls."

Blue looked at Cole for his reaction and he stared back, stone-faced. After several seconds, the two fell over laughing.

During the walk back to the farms, the two of them laughed and convinced themselves that neither person who had mistaken them as both being boys or girls had really looked at them. Cole assured Belinda that no one could mistake her for a boy and likewise, Belinda assured Cole. Someone was approaching, headed toward town, and both of their hearts sank when they saw the looming figure of Tommy.

Cole wasn't sure if Tommy had actually gotten bigger in the two years since the Wrights moved to the Leary farm, but he seemed bigger. Every time he saw Tommy, he not only saw his best friend's tormentor, but he saw his own cowardice and weakness. He would daydream about standing up to him and defending his Blue, but whenever he actually saw Tommy, he hid or walked the other way. There was nowhere to hide now though.

"Well, if it isn't my little brat of a sister with her puny boyfriend," Tommy sneered. He had an angry look and walked straight at them.

Tusk let out a low growl and the fur on his back stood up. They had never seen him do that before.

"We are just going back to the farms," Belinda said, not meeting his gaze and sounding small.

"I didn't ask where you were going, you little shit. But you best get back and do your chores and stop wasting time with this runt."

"I did my chores," Belinda replied without looking up.

Tommy's hand moved quickly and fiercely. He struck Belinda with a thunderous backhand across her face. "Don't backtalk me," he roared, as Belinda staggered and dropped to one knee.

Tusk lurched forward, barking and growling, but Belinda caught him and held him back; she could not bear the thought of him getting hurt too and she knew Tommy would kill a dog even without a reason.

Cole was filled with competing emotions of rage and fear rising within him. He desperately wanted rage to win out, so he opened his mouth and struggled for the words. "Stop hurting her" was all that came out and it came out softly, in a voice that sounded higher and weaker than he had hoped.

"Or what?" Tommy stared down at Cole and stepped forward, raising his fists.

Cole stared at Tommy's big, meaty fists. On his left, he wore a thick brass ring with a cross on it. The irony of the religious symbol struck Cole immediately, as the ring had a smudge of Belinda's blood on it from the backhanded blow. He opened his mouth to answer but was frozen with fear.

Tommy grabbed Cole by the front of his shirt and lifted him off the ground. Then he threw his arms forward, launching Cole through the air. Cole hit the ground hard and, in his fear and confusion, he lost control of himself and felt his short pants dampen.

"Ha! The little runt peed himself," Tommy hooted. "So, Belinda, this is your little boyfriend you spend your time with? This is who you want to kiss? I can't believe you're my sister.

Now get your ass home." Tommy walked past and continued to laugh to himself.

Cole lay there, more embarrassed than hurt, but he could not move for a moment. Belinda came and offered a hand. "I can get up myself," he said, realizing how harsh he sounded.

"I know." She looked at him sadly. As if she knew that this moment, this day, would stay with them forever.

Cole looked back and fought his anger, his hurt pride, and tried to remember she got hit too. She had a bloody cut on her left cheek from Tommy's ring. "We should wash that cut off so you don't get infected," Cole said, trying to talk of anything but his damp pants.

They walked in total silence back to the farms. When they reached Cole's farmhouse, he looked at Belinda and gave a half-hearted wave. He could not muster words. Her blue eyes were moist, and she was not walking away.

Belinda reached out and grabbed Cole's hands. "Bring those short pants tonight and meet me in the trees just past the fence where we first met."

"What?" Cole frowned in confusion. "Why wou—"

"Just trust me." She stepped closer; so close they could feel each other's breath. Her eyes were inches from his own, and he was transfixed.

"OK, Blue."

…

Cole raced into his room to change his clothes, with Tusk at his heels. He was embarrassed enough without his mother, or

Dale, knowing what happened. "You won't tell, will ya, boy?" he said to the dog, as he rubbed both of his scruffy ears. He kept replaying the events of the day, and it seemed worse each time. He felt like hiding in his room forever.

Ma came to the door and asked, "You OK?" Hearing no response, she added, "Belinda OK? Ma had taken a liking to Belinda, and it didn't take much observation to know things were not well in the Wright home, but they had never spoken about it.

"It's fine, Ma."

His mother took her leave and Cole drifted to sleep, with his arms wrapped around Tusk, in a rare afternoon nap. He awoke with a start. He sensed he had been dreaming, but he almost never remembered dreams. Based on the layer of sweat on him, he suspected it wasn't a good dream anyway. There didn't seem much good to dream about today. Evening had come and a gray, dusty light came through his window. He grabbed his short pants and stuffed them into his rucksack and headed for the door. "Ma, I'm headed out for a bit."

"You slept through supper."

"I'll eat when I get back, promise." Cole and Tusk set off to the back field.

...

Stepping through the fence and then into the thicket of trees, he saw his friend had arrived first. "Hi, Blue." He had told himself not to sound glum when he greeted her, to put on a brave face and pretend nothing had happened, but when he heard his own voice, he knew he had failed.

"Hi, Cole." Belinda gave him a muted smile with her lips pressed together.

Looking around in the dim light, he realized the ground was unnatural looking, with little mounds of raised soil all over. He had not noticed that when they met here before.

Belinda held out her hand and said, "Did ya bring 'em?" Her matter-of-fact attitude to this situation was odd but comforting.

"Yeah. In my bag. What are we doing here?"

"My grandma taught me something when I was little. She said, 'Find a place that's all your own; somewhere you are safe. When you have secrets that cause you pain, you can bury those secrets in that special ground, and they can't hurt you anymore.' My grandma was smart, and she saw a lot in her life. She was born all the way over in Ireland and took a boat here when she was my age. I think she had to bury a lot."

Cole remembered Belinda burying the bloody rag. Then his eyes trailed over the lumpy ground and wondered whether her grandma had to bury as much as Belinda herself had. He felt ashamed that his problems were so small by comparison and yet she was helping him bury his pain. "Well, if this is your spot, won't my secret be in the way or something?"

"I think it can be our place now," she said softly, then extended her hand. "Now take 'em out."

Fortunately, the pants were mostly dry when Cole reached into his sack and took them out. He knelt across from Belinda, and they used their hands to scoop out a hole in the mix of pine needles and soil. When they had made the hole large enough, she motioned with a nod of her head for him to drop the pants into the hole. Then they spread the loose ground over them and packed it down.

As Cole pressed down, he felt himself pushing with all his might, as if firmly burying these pants would erase them, and this whole incident, from history. He saw the wisdom in what Belinda's grandma had told her. Belinda put her hands on top of his and helped him press down. Her hands were warm and soft against his, even with the thin layer of slightly moist dirt between them.

They looked at each other, and even in the dying light of dusk, her eyes were so blue that he instinctively called her name softly. "Blue."

She returned his gaze and spoke softly. "You know, my brother is mean and hateful, but he was actually right about one thing." She paused and her eyes darted down and then back up looking into his. "I do want to kiss you."

The warmth in his hands spread to his chest, neck, and face as he felt himself flush. Everything in him wanted to kiss her too, but how had he not thought about it more before this moment? It was as if something was revealed to him that he had always known. They leaned closer and he could feel her breath. His mind raced from first meeting her in this spot, to their shared dog, to his failed bravery.

Then their lips touched, and all went quiet. His upper lip rested above hers so that his two lips held her upper lip as softly as hers held his lower lip. They did not move and just held the perfect moment. Cole felt that he could stay in this exact place forever. An hour earlier he wanted to hide in his room forever, now he wanted to kiss Belinda forever. Things happen for a reason, he thought. Their lips released and she smiled at him, her eyes bright. They both knew that this really would be the moment, the day, they remembered forever.

March 1850 – Cold Spring, New York

*L*ife on the farm rolled on. Ma was a force and could ne-
gotiate prices for her crops as well as any man. She still
had no interest in men at all, though a few of the older men
in the area had tried. They'd bring a gift, and she would say
something like 'How thoughtful' and close the door and leave
them outside, hat in hand.

Dale had married a girl in 1848 to the shock of everyone, as
no one had ever seen him actually talk with her. He just went
one day to her father and asked permission. To this day Ma and
Cole were not sure whether their new in-law, Katherine, even
knew Dale before he did that, but she went along with it in any
case, and now they seemed happy enough.

Katherine was a chatterbox and always smiling. She talked a
mile a minute while Dale would nod and gesture, often at the
right times, but not always. Then she would playfully slap the
back of her hand to his chest and say, "aren't you listenin'?" Cole
said to Ma, on the day of their wedding, "You know, between
the two of them, they smile and talk about the right amount
for a regular couple."

Ma worked hard to hold back a laugh and said, "Don't tease
about your brother on his day."

Katherine's family had a farm as well, and Dale built a small house for them right next to her parents'. Her dad might have assumed that he now had another farmhand, but Dale kept showing up at Ma's every morning and working. Ma always said that the farm would be the boys' to run someday, but they all assumed it would be Dale's. He really had no desire to be anywhere else. Katherine was expecting their first child and was positively glowing about it. Even Dale had a prideful look that might have even verged on joy.

At seventeen, Cole was now finally taller than Belinda, but barely. He remained stick skinny but strong, with lean muscles that now showed when he worked in the fields. Cole's dark hair was cut now and hung down to his ears. His narrow face had filled out, but his features were still sharp. His dark eyes under thick eyebrows gave him an intense, serious look when he was thoughtful, but when he smiled, which was most often, he wore his happiness in every crease on his face.

Belinda had fair skin, but her freckles would darken when she got sun in the fields. Her shoulder-length dirty blonde hair still lightened as it descended to her shoulders. She retained a hint of her tomboy look from years prior, but she was undeniably beautiful. Her brilliant blue eyes were intelligent and curious. The freckles on her nose drew attention to a kind face that struck a balance between being delicate and strong. She was slim but her body had filled out with narrow but more womanly hips and breasts that were proportioned to her slim figure and shapely.

For Cole and Belinda, in some ways, nothing had changed and in others everything had. They were still the closest of friends, spending every spare moment together. Ma would tell Cole he should make other friends too, but he never saw the point. Belinda filled every need he had. They laughed together; shared, and buried, secrets together; and they nursed Belinda's regular injuries together. She was his friend, his love, and his family all in one.

What changed and grew over the years was their passion. Their first kiss had ignited a flame that grew and was never quenched. They managed to limit themselves to kissing, more and more passionately, for about a year. They knew, from sermons and gossip, that it would be a sin, or unrespectable, to do more. But by the time they were fourteen, the dam broke and they began exploring each other's bodies. A new line was created in their minds that they could remain respectable by not having sex.

The new line left a lot of room for them to explore and enjoy each other, and by age fifteen they imagined that they had done everything that one could possibly do with another's body, many times, but without having sex. In the two years since then, they had held out, not out of some concern for respectability, but for fear of pregnancy. Belinda would joke to Cole, "Well, I think respectability left on the train a while back."

It was a beautiful March day in the Hudson Valley. A few large, puffy, white clouds hung motionless in an otherwise bright blue sky. Cole and Belinda walked the dirt road toward town, talking about all of the new houses along the way. The area had grown in the past years, with more farmers clearing the fertile land. As a result, more commerce popped up too. The town had stores for clothes, a small inn, and the general store had doubled in size. There was even a playhouse opening a few towns over.

They passed the spot where Tommy had struck Belinda and thrown Cole to the ground years earlier and they both went quiet for a moment.

"My daddy is dying," Belinda said softly.

"Oh, Blue, I'm sorry." Cole didn't feel a sense of surprise, though he was sorry for her. Whatever kind of man her father was; he was her daddy. He had been drinking hard for years. At first, he would just show signs of being drunk, staggering into town or church, but then he started to look yellowish, and finally, he just wasn't seen around town at all. Despite all that they shared with one another, they never really talked about their dads.

Belinda stopped and turned to Cole. "The doc came to the house and said there's nothing he can do. Daddy drank too much for too long. I feel bad saying it, but I don't really know if I'll miss him. It's not like he really talked to me much. He was just kind of *there*."

"Well, at least he was *there*. My daddy left."

It was the first time she had heard this. Cole had always told her his daddy was gone and he did not want to talk about it. She thought he had died. She did not know what to say.

"I'm sorry, Blue, this isn't about my daddy. I really am sorry for you."

Her eyes filled with tears as she said, "It's selfish of me, but what I am really afraid of is that Tommy will get even worse."

It hadn't occurred to Cole that Tommy's malice was hindered

at all by his sickly, drunken father, but perhaps the idea of him being the official man of the house would unleash his violence even more. Over the past years, Tommy had become more volatile. He had disappeared for a few months in 1849, and they had hoped he went west with the news of gold in California. But he returned, and it seemed he was meaner than ever. Rumor was that he had taken up with a married woman, but it ended when he'd given her a terrible beating.

In truth, they had never known of Tommy having a girlfriend. One girl in the next town accused him of rape but her father put an end to it for fear of shame on his family. In this small-town area, most people knew Tommy was trouble and smart girls stayed away.

Tommy seemed to hate everyone, but he had a special level of malice for his sister and Cole. They had to stay out of his way when spending time together. The mere sight of the two of them together would send him into a fury and Belinda would get the worst of it later at home.

Realizing his face likely gave away his fear of Tommy becoming the head of Wright household, Cole shook his head quickly and said, "Nah, it will be fine." But he didn't believe that, and Belinda knew it.

Three days later, Emit Wright passed. With only three people to work the farm for the past months—Tommy, Belinda, and their mother—the Wrights were poor, and the funeral showed it. They did not buy a coffin, but instead buried him in two grain sacks. One pulled down over his head and the other up from his feet. Belinda stitched the sacks together at his waist.

Her mother had picked a place on their property to bury him, not too far from the house, just away from the wooded thicket, so the sun would shine on him most of the day—Tommy dug a deep hole for the body. It was precariously close to the wooded area where Belinda buried her secrets, but no one saw her dirt mounds within the trees.

Cole and Ma came, as did Dale and Katherine and a few more folks from town. The priest stood at the graveside and greeted those in attendance, reminding them of the time for mass that Sunday.

The day was beautiful and felt so contrary to the severity of the moment. The sun shone brightly; a light breeze rustled the leaves and birds were singing. The sun was directly in Cole's face; it felt warm and reassuring. How could they be dealing with death in such a moment? Maybe, he thought, it was a sign of better times to come. He heard the priest say something about controlling one's demons, a thinly veiled nod to Emit Wright's drinking that did him in.

Belinda moved next to Cole and whispered, "I guess there is no secret being buried today."

"I'm so sorry, Blue," Cole said softly, as he held her left hand in both of his.

He looked up and met Tommy's eye and it startled him. The sun beamed behind the large man, making him almost glow around his silhouette and creating a dark shadow of his facial features. He always saw hatred and venom in Belinda's brother, but this was different; worse. There was murder in his eyes. He could not say how he knew, but he felt it.

The priest concluded and released the small crowd to "go with God." The crowd milled about, offering condolences to the family. Alice and Buck stood by, looking more confused than sad. The women in the group all patted the kids' heads and whispered, "There, there." Mrs. Wright accepted the condolences and smiled sheepishly, looking as lost and confused as her younger children.

Cole approached Mrs. Wright and said, "I am sorry for your loss, Ma'am."

She looked nervously at him and then shifted her eyes to Tommy who was approaching. "You best go, please," she said in a cracked, shaky voice.

Cole felt his usual fear rise and he turned swiftly. He saw Belinda hurrying to go with him, but Tommy grabbed her arm and she let out a short, involuntary yelp of pain.

"Where do you think you're going?" Tommy said through gritted teeth as he tightened his grip and Belinda winced.

Cole stepped forward; a flurry of thoughts rushing through his head; was this the moment his courage would surmount his fear? His eyes darted around for a weapon, and he saw the shovel that waited to refill the grave. A plan formed in his head. He took one step toward the shovel and was suddenly face to face with Ma. She had stepped into his path quickly.

With her hands on his chest, Ma said, "Not here, son."

"But …" As his senses came to him, he looked around at the small, dispersing crowd. Their eyes were on Tommy, shaking their heads. He saw the empty grave; the priest; Mrs. Wright.

He was on Tommy's land and there were more than a dozen witnesses. His mother was right. He had to walk away.

…

They walked home in silence. Katherine started to speak at one point, but Dale placed a hand on her shoulder and shook his head. Cole could not shake what he saw in Tommy's eyes; he feared for Belinda.

They arrived at the farmhouse and Tusk, who was tied up outside, greeted them with a wag, but quickly stopped and whined at them, sensing the mood. Tusk rarely left Cole's side, but Ma had said the funeral was no place for a dog. Cole untied Tusk and pulled him firmly into his arms. The dog obliged and laid his head by Cole's neck. Cole whispered, "Tell me what to do, boy." Tusk just looked at him and cocked his head at the questioning tone.

They all quietly filed into the house and took seats; Katherine in the rocking chair, the rest on stools, and Tusk lying at Cole's feet. After a few minutes of silence, Katherine couldn't take it and said, "Well, the service was nice." She paused and added quietly, "'til the end, anyway."

Cole managed a partial smile at his sister-in-law. He often thought of her as silly and lacking substance. He didn't see in her the strength that Ma or Belinda had, but she was kind and his brother loved her.

That evening they ate a quiet supper of roasted chicken, potatoes, and beets. After dinner, as the evening wore on, conversation between Ma, Dale, and Katherine returned to normal.

They talked of the baby's arrival, of course, and what their future plans would be. Ma brought out the neutral beige sweater she'd been knitting for the little one, and she and Katherine talked excitedly about whether it would be a boy or girl. Dale, being characteristically brief said, "I assume it'll be one of those," and gave a little smile.

Tusk gave a low growl, followed by a whimpering cry. "What is it, boy?" Cole asked. The dog then ran to the front door and started pawing at it madly, as if he were digging a hole in the vertical surface. He cried loudly and seemed to be in a panic.

Cole went to open the door, but Ma said, "Hold on." She darted into her room and emerged with a rifle. It was her husband's hunting rifle that had been dormant since he had left. "Go on now. Let 'em out and let's see what he's after."

By the time the door was open just a few inches, the dog frantically pushed through and bounded down the four steps in a single leap. He tore across the yard toward the field and stopped, nuzzling at a lump on the ground. They could not make out what it was from the porch.

Cole sprinted down the steps and across the yard. Ma followed then Dale came, shouting back to Katherine to stay on the porch. As Cole reached Tusk, his heart sank to see Belinda collapsed on the ground. She was on her left side, with her knees pulled to her chest. Her shirt was torn, and the pale moonlight illuminated partially dried blood caked on the right side of her face. Her right eye was completely closed with a bulge of swelling the size of a crab apple. She held her right side and her breathing was labored and wheezy. For a moment, Cole didn't want to touch her, it felt like she would disintegrate in his grasp. In that moment he feared she could be dying, and his thoughts flashed to the murderous look in Tommy's eyes.

He knelt at her side and placed a hand gently on her shoulder. She immediately recoiled and gasped with pain at the motion. Tusk gently licked her face, making a clean patch in the blood. "Blue," Cole said in a whisper. Ma and Dale had joined behind Cole and were dumbstruck. "Blue," Cole said again, slightly louder. "I'm so sorry I left you there." He realized he was weeping now and drops of tears were joining the blood on her cheek. "I'll never let this happen again."

Ma broke from her trance and said, "We need to get her inside and cleaned up." Regaining her wits, she took control. "Dale, get a bed quilt we'll use to carry her. Tell Katherine to boil some water and drag Cole's mattress out into the family area. Cole, you stay right where you are and keep talking to her. Dale will ride to fetch the doc once we have her inside."

Dale returned with the quilt, and they laid it behind Belinda. Slowly, they rolled her onto it as she winced with pain. Dale and Ma each grabbed a corner by her feet and Cole took the end by her head and grabbed both corners. They lifted her easily, and she nestled in the makeshift stretcher as they walked her back to the house.

As they laid her on the mattress, her torn shirt fell open and they could see an angry welt on the side of her ribs. Cole hurried to cover her exposed breast with the quilt, though that type of modesty didn't seem very important at the moment. With the light of two lanterns in the room, her face looked worse than it had outside. It was contorted so much by swelling that Cole was not sure how he even knew for sure that this was his Blue.

Dale left to get the doc, taking their cart horse to get to town quickly. Ma and Katherine dipped clean linen into the boiled water and wrung it out. "We need to undress her, Cole," Ma said. "Get the shears from the barn, as I suspect we won't get that shirt off without hurting her worse." She laid a warm, wet linen on Belinda's face and let it soak there. The back of it immediately turned maroon, soaking through with her blood.

Cole returned with the sheers and Ma held out her hand. He shook his head, "No—I need to do this." He bent down and gently started cutting away the fabric. When he had all of the shirt off of her, with only the back still underneath her, they laid the wet linens on her side. She winced with even the slightest touch. He leaned down and let his lips just graze a place near her ear that looked unhurt and whispered, "I love you, Blue."

The faintest smile appeared on her bloodied, swollen lips.

Doc Blackwell was a quiet man, bald on top with a circle of short dark hair around his head. He was slim and hunched over at the shoulders. His wire glasses sat halfway down a sharp nose. He moved quickly through the house and stood over Belinda. He made a tsking sound with his lips, showing his disapproval of what had happened to her.

"You've done well to clean her and get her comfortable," he began, as he assessed her situation. "The face will heal. I'm more worried about the ribs and her lungs." He leaned over her and placed a hand on her side, pressing slightly, which elicited a yelp of pain from Belinda. Tusk cried in the corner. "She has several broken ribs. I'll need to listen to her lungs." He proceeded to take a tool from his bag that none of them had seen before. It was a metal disc, like a coin, with a tube attached to it at one end and had a flange at the other. He explained, "This is the latest stethoscope, used in New York City." It was clear he was proud to have one as a country doctor. "I can hear more clearly with this than the old wooden stethoscope." He placed the metal disc on Belinda's chest and the flange over his ear. His brow furrowed deeply, and his glasses slid down his nose as he strained to hear.

He stood and turned toward Ma. She nodded to Cole in a motion conveying that the doctor should address him. He obliged and turned to Cole. "She's obviously been badly beaten, as you can see. Her face will heal. I can't be sure if any bones broke in her cheek, but there is nothing we can do for those anyway, other than let them heal. The ribs are badly broken. Her breathing is constricted by the ribs and will cause her great pain for a month or more, but I don't think the lung was punctured. She can stay home, on bed rest. Keep her head elevated to help avoid pneumonia. I'll call on her in a few days. Will she be at the Wright farmhouse?"

Cole hesitated at the question. He opened his mouth to speak but Ma beat him to it, saying firmly, "She will be here."

Cole heard the resolve in his mother's voice. He looked at her and she seemed larger to him. Her back was straight, and she had an air of certainty. Ma had decided something in that moment, but he didn't know what.

The next morning, Dale did not come to the house. Ma had declared that farm work would be on hold for a week. She moved briskly around the house, making breakfast, checking on Belinda's wounds. The rifle she had retrieved the night before stayed by the door.

Belinda woke, still in the middle of the family room, and looked around as if trying to recall how she had arrived here. She was on a mattress, propped up with rolled blankets that elevated her head and chest. Cole was in the rocking chair by her side, where he had spent the entire night. Seeing her eyes open, he slid down and knelt beside her. Her right eye was completely closed by red, raw swelling but her left looked up at him. He saw the bright blue and watched a tear roll out of the edge and streak down her left cheek. She managed a slight curl to her lips in a feeble smile.

"Doc says you'll be OK." Cole tried to look as confident and reassuring as he could. "Do you remember anything from last night? Never mind that, don't talk. That was dumb of me. Let me just tell you something. I love you, Blue, and I swear to you on my life that Tommy's never going to hurt you again. We'll get the sheriff over here later, and if he won't help, I'll kill Tommy myself." Belinda put her hand on his arm, and he realized he was talking faster and louder as he went on. The touch told him this wasn't what she needed right now. "Well, let me get you some water and soft eggs." Cole stood and shuffled from the room.

That afternoon Belinda sat up more. They had pulled the mattress to the wall, which made it easier for her to sit up and prop herself against the wall with the rolled blankets behind her. Ma brought warm tea with honey. She had boiled extra water and brought a pot with a cloth and started washing the dried blood from Belinda's hair. She asked, "Would you like the sheriff to come by? I know the law doesn't always help in family matters, but he'd at least talk with Tommy and put a scare in him."

Belinda shook her head. Cole started to protest but Ma caught his eye and gave a slight shake of her head, and he held his tongue.

When Ma returned to the kitchen to dump the bloody water, Cole followed. "Ma, without the sheriff, he'll just keep doing this 'til he kills her."

She put a hand on his chest. "We aren't going to let that happen."

Something in her response reassured him but he was still worried. The future had never been so unclear to him. He always knew he would spend his life with Belinda; they would be happy forever together. Now, that future seemed hazy; the ground under his feet felt unstable.

…

Three days passed before Doc Blackwell appeared again at the door. He shuffled in, toting his brown leather bag. He looked at Ma, then without being prompted, turned to Cole and asked, "How's our girl doing?"

"She is mending well, sir. She's the strongest person I know."

The doctor smiled and nodded, then went to the room in the back to examine Belinda. Her hair was clean, and they'd managed to get her into one of Ma's nightdresses. The swelling had receded enough to open her right eye to a slit, but the bruising was now a fierce-looking purple, surrounded by a yellow tinge.

He touched the side of her face lightly and examined the eye, saying, "Good, good," almost to himself.

Belinda was able to lean forward and drop the loose-fitting nightdress down over both shoulders to reveal her broken right side. The doctor asked about pain, and she managed a crooked smile, "It only hurts when I breathe."

Satisfied with what he had seen, Doc rose to his feet and declared to all three of them, "She's on the mend. Keep quiet and still for the next month, young lady. Any upset to those ribs could be deadly. I hate to call you lucky after such a trauma, but indeed this might have ended worse. I pray you'll stay safe."

It was obvious to them all that his unspoken advice was *Stay away from your brother.* Everyone in town knew what had happened, and who had done it, by now.

That evening, Dale and Katherine came to dinner. Cole sat on the floor next to Belinda and they slid the table over, so it was almost like they were sitting around it together. As usual, Katherine dominated the conversation, but Belinda was back to talking and even lightly laughing, though she held her side each time she did. Dale rarely spoke, as normal, while Ma pretended to be herself, but Cole could see she was thinking about what was to come. Tusk gave a low growl and looked to the door.

Cole rose and walked to the door and Ma followed. The room went so silent they could all hear the steady chirp of crickets outside that none had noticed until now. Cole went to open the door, but Ma said, "Hold on." She took the rifle that leaned by the door in her hands, stepped back a few paces, and said, "OK. Open it slowly." Cole opened the door a crack. There was no one on the porch. He felt the pounding of his heart as if it were trying to break free from his chest. He opened it wider with a creak and stepped out. In the shadows in front of the house, he saw the small figure of Maye Wright step forward.

Ma returned the gun to its place propped against the entry wall and stepped out. "Hello, Maye. Have you come to see Belinda?"

The woman shifted her feet and looked around as if she were searching for the words to respond somewhere in the night air around her. There was a long silence, but Ma didn't give her the relief of adding words to the moment, she just waited. At long last she spoke, and her voice was soft and shaky, "Well, I've come to fetch her."

"She needs to mend, Maye. Can't travel just yet, but you're welcome in if you'd like."

Mrs. Wright glanced over toward the side of the house and nervously shook her head, then stammered, "My-my girl's place is at home. I-I've come to fetch her."

Ma put a hand on Cole's chest, gently urging him back into the doorway. She took a step back as well. "Like I said, Maye, she's not fit for travel. Come in if you like, but Belinda stays where she's at." Then she added as an afterthought, "Doc's orders."

Cole was awed by his mother's intuition and intelligence. By saying "Doc's orders," she conveyed that she was not taking this woman's daughter of her own volition. He heard movement from the side of the house and knew it had to be Tommy. Cole and Ma went inside and barred the door.

They remained quiet for an hour. Tusk's low growl had

subsided after fifteen minutes, and they assumed Tommy had gone. For safety's sake, Dale and Katherine decided to stay the night and took Cole's room. Ma slept with the rifle at her side.

Cole and Belinda lay on the mattress in the family room, staring up at the ceiling, with Tusk curled up at their feet.

"Tell me about your daddy, Cole," Belinda asked while he stroked her hair.

"What brought that on?"

"I guess my daddy dying, and it's just the only secret you've ever kept from me."

"Well, how would you know about my other secrets … they're secret," Cole said, flashing a wry smile. The smile faded slowly, and his face became drawn. He looked pale and his head tilted down slightly. "He just left. Ma never talks about it. Dale says there was another woman, but I don't know; I wasn't even ten yet. He was a good dad, I thought. He never beat on us boys, and sometimes we probably deserved to be." Cole swallowed and tears filled his eyes. He turned away from Belinda.

She reached out and turned him back toward her, saying, "I think we are way past having to turn away from each other." Then she gently wiped his tear with her thumb.

"I just don't understand why he did it; he made a vow to Ma, 'til death; he had two boys. He seemed happy to me, but I don't really know, I guess."

A tear escaped Belinda's swollen right eye. "My daddy left us too. He just did it slower. He drank so much he was never really there anyway. I don't really know what's worse—leaving or quitting." She paused and looked toward the bedrooms. "At least you've got her. My mama is so weak and beaten. I don't even blame her or hate her. She's kind of like my daddy. She didn't take to drinking but she quit all the same."

"Blue, I need you to know something." Cole put a hand on each of her cheeks and stared deeply at her with his pitch-dark eyes. "I'm not like my daddy. I won't quit and I won't ever leave you. I hate that half my blood is from that quitter, and I just need you to know. When we get married, it's a promise that we never leave each other."

Belinda held his face now and looked deep into his eyes. "Well, if that's what marriage is—a promise to never leave each other—I figure me and you've been married for years already … in all the ways that really matter." She managed a full smile.

There was no holding back the tears now; no looking away. Cole leaned his streaked face in. "I love you more than anything in the world, Blue." He kissed her gently. He laid down close along her left side and they drifted to sleep.

…

The house was awakened by Tusk barking and snarling at the front door. Cole jumped to his feet and Ma ran out holding the rifle. Dale came out behind them but waved for Katherine to stay in the room. Ma motioned with the rifle for Cole to unlatch the door. First, he picked up Tusk, who tried to wiggle free, and brought him to Belinda. She soothed the dog and held him firmly.

The front hall was a short, clear path to the door. Ma stood with the rifle pointed straight at the center. Cole inched up the side, conscious of staying out of the line of fire, and unbarred the door. He heard the creak of the front porch under heavy feet and knew Tommy stood on the other side. He swung the door open and stepped back. Tommy stood in the doorway, his nose must have been almost pressed to the door, based on how close he was. His broad frame nearly blocked the entire opening; only thin streaks of the moonlit night peered in around him.

"Give me my sister, now," Tommy growled with a finger pointed at Cole.

Steadying the rifle to aim at Tommy's chest, Ma said calmly, "You know if you trespass, I can shoot you dead, and right now, you are one step from trespassing."

Cole stayed frozen, as amazed by his mother as he was afraid of Tommy.

Tommy's face turned red and through gritted teeth, he hissed, "That's my kin and she belongs to me and you've got no right."

"Doc's orders," Ma said calmly.

"Well, how about sheriff's orders. I'll get the law. You know she'll have to come home then." Tommy's face shifted to a grin full of malice, as he seemed pleased with his own wits.

There was a loud click and Cole turned to see Ma cock the gun. Tommy's face dropped. Ma remained quiet and calm and said, "Now you go ahead and get the law. I'd be happy to explain that I've hired this young woman on my farm." Cole, Belinda, and Dale stared in amazement as they listened to this revelation. "She's seventeen and can decide her own work. We made a deal and she's staying here. The sheriff will be happy to explain to you that you can't interfere with my labor. You so much as look at her, or ever set foot on my property again, and I'll do more than point this rifle, and the law will be on my side."

Tommy turned beet red, his hands balled in fists and shaking at his sides. He picked up one foot as if to step inside but stared down the barrel of that rifle and turned and stomped off. As he went down the stairs, he kicked the left newel post so hard that it cracked in the center and the railing listed to the left.

Cole closed and barred the door. Katherine emerged from the bedroom, wide-eyed. They all stared at Ma, with wonder and no small amount of admiration. Ma lowered the rifle, only now showing signs of shaking hands. She thumped it straight down, leaned on it like a walking stick, and let out a heavy breath.

The first to speak was Belinda, her bruised face creasing with a smile. "Well, boss, what are my new duties on the farm?" They all let out a laugh, and Dale, Cole, and Katherine surrounded and hugged Ma so tightly that she disappeared from Belinda's view inside the circle of her grateful kids. Despite the triumph, no one felt safe; no one felt this was over. Just for the moment, there was relief.

…

A month passed, and work on the farm had resumed fully. Ma had set out some basic rules for safety. Belinda was only to work the near field, so as not to be seen from the Wright farm, and they were to work in pairs, always. Whoever was working with Belinda would have the rifle. But as the days passed, the feeling of impending danger lessened, and they began to hope that Tommy would not return.

It was midafternoon on a warm late-April Wednesday. Cole and Belinda were taking one of their regular afternoon breaks behind the barn to practice their skills at giving each other pleasure without risking pregnancy. Laying behind the barn, the smell of hay carried on the light breeze. Cole's head rested on Belinda's bare stomach. Her shirt was open, and his right hand rested on her left breast, softly stroking. "Blue, we aren't going to live our life on this farm. We'll need to find our own place someday."

She cocked her head to look into his eyes. "What made you think about that now?"

"It's just that Katherine will have the baby soon, and this'll be Dale's farm someday. He's the oldest. He'd share it if I asked but I don't want to live with my brother forever. And of course, we have to be on guard all the time here with Tommy close by."

"Where would we go? Do I have to leave what's left of my family? I miss Alice and Buck. They've got no daddy now. Tommy's never hurt them, he seems to save that for me, but I fear he will. Mama is no use at all. I just don't know what'll become of them and I can't go over there to see."

"What if we took the little ones with us? We could head west. There's farmland and even gold."

"I don't know, Cole. Do we need to decide before we tend the weeds this afternoon? Or, maybe we can meet in this spot tomorrow, and the next day, and the one after that, and talk more about it. After I have my fun with you, of course." She gave him a smile and scrunched the skin on her nose with the playful look that he loved.

August 1850 – Cold Spring, New York

By August the family hardly thought about Tommy Wright anymore. They still adhered to Ma's rules, but four months felt like a long time, given that Tommy lived less than a half mile away and could have come any time.

Belinda was sleeping on Dale's mattress that they had pulled into Ma's bedroom. Ma knew that Belinda and Cole snuck away to do whatever they did together, but she was still determined that under her roof an unmarried couple would not stay in the same bed.

It was a late August Monday afternoon and Alice and Buck were at the Thomas farm, visiting Belinda. They had started coming by the farm to see her for the past several weeks. She was always thrilled to see them, and their bond was growing again to what it was when she lived at home. Alice was now eleven, the same age Belinda and Cole were when they met. She was heavier set than her sister and almost as tall. Her light brown hair was curly and fell around a round face with full cheeks. Despite their differing builds, there was a sisterly similarity between them. She was attractive and friendly looking but bore a sadness in her eyes that seemed to disappear when she saw her big sister.

Buck was a slim, small nine-year-old with sandy straight hair and as many freckles as Belinda. He moved fast and spoke excitedly about everything. It made the words sometimes come out so fast that he'd have to repeat himself and slow down for people to understand him.

Alice took Belinda's hand and said, "We ain't seen Tommy in a few weeks. No one knows where he went and work's piling up at the farm."

"You *haven't* seen Tommy," Belinda corrected, then quickly changed the subject, as she did not want to talk of her brother. "How is school; and how is Mama?"

Alice ignored the first part of the question, "Mama sleeps later now, and when she does get up, she barely speaks. I guess I should say she barely does anything. I've been making Buck his breakfast and washing his clothes. No farm work's been done since Tommy left."

Belinda was worried but tried not to show it as her younger siblings looked at her expectantly. "It will work out. I'm sure Tommy will come back and work the fields, or Mama will hire a farmhand." She wasn't sure she believed it, and even though the family needed Tommy's labor to make it at the farm, she wished deeply that he would never return. It felt like an unworthy wish, but she couldn't help herself.

After Alice and Buck left the farm, Belinda took Cole behind the barn. They knelt in the grass and started to kiss passionately. Cole started to pull her sundress up, but she stopped him. "Before all that …" She smiled at him. "I want to talk to you."

"OK." He looked at her with a hint of concern in his dark eyes.

"It's nothing bad, and I will get you out of your clothes soon," she smiled, but then the smile trailed away, and she held his gaze. "I can't stay imprisoned here forever."

"Imprisoned? How can you say …"

"Hold on. I don't mean it that way. You and your mother aren't my jailers; you've been my saviors. We both know I'd probably be dead if I'd gone back. But I *am* trapped here. I haven't left this farm in four months. I'm not going to live my entire life on fifteen acres of land, guarded by a rifle against an enemy on the other side of our fence."

"I know. We just haven't figured out where to go and with what money."

"Wait." She placed a hand on Cole's chest and gave a look begging patience with her story. "I didn't say anything about going away either. Running seems no better than hiding, and I don't want to leave Alice and Buck." She paused and looked carefully at him. "Our fathers were quitters; we aren't."

"So, what are you saying?" Cole looked at her appraisingly. He was used to having answers come easily to him, but this time the problem was beyond him.

"I'm saying that we are going to town on Saturday; we're going to get ice cream; we're going to walk together; I'm going to church with you and Ma on Sunday; I'm going to check on Alice and Buck and Mama at the farm; and we are going to live our lives."

Cole could see there was no argument to make here. His mind rolled through problems with her plan and potential modifications to keep her safe, in case Tommy showed up, but then he decided to just nod in agreement.

"And one more thing," Belinda added, looking at him with desire, sliding a hand down his chest, and then unbuttoning his jeans. "We have waited years to make love like a married couple. We've been afraid I'd get pregnant before we had a plan to raise a family and how we would live. Well, after church your mother usually stays in town for a while. You and I will come straight home, and we will love each other fully. I don't care if I get pregnant."

Cole stared, speechless. After a moment he swallowed and just smiled at her. He thought to himself that this woman was as forceful and brave as she was beautiful. He wished Sunday were not six days away.

Belinda smiled, reading his thoughts, and said, "Now, where were we?" She pulled her sundress off over her head in a single motion and knelt, naked, before him.

...

Saturday came and it was a scorching hot day with full sun and no breeze. Cole and Belinda walked slowly, hand-in-hand, on the dirt road toward the center of Cold Spring. Cole had expected to feel more trepidation, but when this day came, he set out confident they would make it without incident. They laughed and talked along the way and suddenly Cole realized they had already passed the place where Tommy had hit Belinda and humiliated him. He thought with satisfaction that perhaps he really had buried that history.

Small beads of sweat formed on Belinda's forehead and trickled down, dropping occasionally from the end of her nose. Her left hand, holding Cole's right, with interlaced fingers, was wet but neither of them minded.

As they approached the general store, they saw a small crowd out front. The mood seemed jovial, with hoots and cheers occasionally ringing out. Cole looked at Belinda and shrugged the unspoken suggestion to go check it out. She nodded back.

In the center of a circle of rapt listeners was Joseph Mills, a boy from town a few years older than Cole but younger than Dale. They had heard he'd gone west with the earliest of those seeking gold, back at the end of 1848, but it hardly seemed possible that he could have made it all that way to California and back, so Cole immediately wondered if he got turned back by some misfortune.

He held in his hand a gold nugget the size of his fist and continued his story. "All in all, it took me half a year to reach California, but only four months on the way home. I was motivated to get back to the greatest little town in the world." With that, the eager crowd let out another whoop.

"I'll tell you though, I was lucky to have gone early. I found fortune in the first two months. I kept trying for more, but prospectors kept coming from everywhere and the pickins got slimmer. It was like a swarm of bees. By late April, I decided to quit while the quittin' was good and take what I got back home. Besides, I missed my mama." At that, a forty-something woman planted a big kiss on his cheek and the crowd gave a jeering *Awww.*

"Anyway, folks, I'm sure glad to be home, but I set out to New York City come Wednesday to cash out there. I'll take this nugget" —he gave a wink— "along with the rest, with me. Out west, there were too many folks looking to swindle, and I wanted to take my gold home for payment."

Joseph walked away and the crowd clamored with excitement. Cole heard one of the older men in the crowd exclaim, "A real live prospector who struck gold, standing right here in Cold Spring." Another replied, "And he'll fetch more'n twenty dollars for each ounce."

They entered the store, stepping through excited townspeople, and ordered their ice cream. They sat on the stoop eating; there was limited conversation, with most of their concentration on managing their rapidly melting desserts.

They finished and started to walk back, hand-in-hand again. Cole was lost in thought. Belinda gave him a bit of a nudge and said, "Hello over there."

"Sorry, Blue. I was just thinking what it must have been like going all the way to California. Six months of rugged travel but then seeing it pay off like that. He'll be able to buy land, build a house, and support a family."

"He took a big risk though," She countered. "A lot of folks don't survive a trip like that. Outlaws on the path, snakes, cold. There're more things that could kill you than you can count. And I bet you most folks who go looking for gold don't find it."

Hearing the concern in her voice, Cole smiled and said, "It's just a neat story, Blue, that's all. I've got my gold right here." He pulled her close and kissed her firmly, with one hand on her lower back pressing her into his body and the other one on the back of her head, stroking her hair.

When they released the kiss, she said, "You'd best believe that." They walked home kicking rocks past each other in the game they had made up so many years ago.

…

Ma, Cole, and Belinda stepped into church on Sunday morning, seeing Dale and Katherine already there. Katherine looked like she could pop with a pinprick to her belly. She was due any day and this oppressive heat made her look as if she were melting. But she greeted them with a smile nonetheless and began talking about how ready she was to have this baby.

Cole and Belinda listened politely, but both of their minds were on their plans for after the service. They felt the anticipation for a moment and a day they would remember for the rest of their lives.

Maye Wright walked in with Alice and Buck in tow. She looked as if she had just awoken. Her hair was unkempt, and her shirt hung on her bony shoulders, revealing an alarming loss of weight. Ma and Cole had seen some decline in prior weeks, but this was stark. Belinda had not seen her mother in four months and stood open-mouthed in horror. She immediately thought of what Alice had told her. She had brushed it off too casually and felt a pang of guilt.

Alice met Belinda's eye and they exchanged looks that conveyed they both understood each other now. Belinda steeled her nerves and approached her mother. "Mama," she said so softly it seemed she feared the breath from her words could knock her over.

Mrs. Wright looked up with hollow eyes and said, "Oh, hello, dear," then walked past like a ghost and sat in the first pew she arrived at.

Belinda reached out to Alice and Buck and gently squeezed their arms. "We'll figure this out together, OK?" They nodded and everyone took their seats for the procession.

Mass ended and Cole looked into Belinda's blue eyes with a desire that he felt sinful for, here in a house of God. He took her hand to walk out; lead her home and into a new phase of their lives. There would always be a before and after this day. Then he heard a sharp cry. He spun around to see Katherine in the middle of the church aisle, standing with legs awkwardly apart, as if she were riding an invisible horse. A puddle of water soaked the floor beneath her and more trickled down her legs.

Dale stood, bewildered and frozen. He looked from Katherine to Ma. Ma said, "Her water's broke; time to have a baby." As always, she knew how to take control and she started setting orders out, "Cole, our farm is closer than their home, so we will go there. Katherine's parents and Doc Blackwell are probably just out the door. Go fetch them and have them join us at the farm. Belinda, you run on ahead and get some fresh water from the pump and set it to boil. Dale, you stay right with Katherine and help her walk."

Everyone hesitated a moment, then Ma clapped her hands. "Let's go." At that, they all sprung to their assigned tasks.

Later that afternoon, a baby girl joined the family. Katherine was brave throughout, and Doc Blackwell said the baby was perfect. Dale muddled through the birth in a fog but now he was beaming. They named her Eleanore Jane Thomas, using the names of both maternal grandmothers, who had passed years ago. Doc suggested that Katherine not move for a few days, so Dale and Katherine took Cole's room, and he would sleep in the family room.

As the activity died down and evening crept over the farm, Cole and Belinda sat on the front steps. The heat of the day had passed, and a mild evening air blew softly across the corn, now too tall to see over. The first stars were starting to peer out and there was a steady hum of crickets.

Belinda leaned her head on Cole's shoulder, and he kissed the top of her head. He had expected today to be one that he'd remember for the rest of his life, and even though it took an unexpected turn, he was right. He did not consider himself religious at all. In fact, his mother would joke, whenever he asked pointed questions or called Christianity into question, "You are a Thomas for sure," a reference that their name coincided with the apostle who refused to believe in the resurrection without proof. But Cole saw meaning in the timing of events. He felt today's events prevented him from being with Belinda for a purpose. What that purpose was, he didn't know.

"Not the day we planned, huh, Blue?"

Belinda smiled. "It's such a miracle though. There's a person in the world who wasn't here this morning, and we're going to know her all her life. I wonder what she'll be like."

"I suppose she'll either talk all the time or not at all." Cole laughed.

"You are terrible."

"I know. Did you see Dale tonight, though? I've never seen him that happy or proud. I think he'll be a good father."

Belinda got serious. "Did you see my mama?" She felt the sudden change of subject and was sorry to ruin the festive mood, but she was afraid for Alice and Buck. "Alice tried to tell me, but I didn't understand how bad it was. I need to do something."

"What are you going to do?"

"I'm going over there tomorrow. I have to see how things are."

"What about Tommy?"

"They haven't seen him in weeks, and like I said, I'm going to live my life. That includes caring for my family."

Cole nodded. "I know better than to try to change your mind, but I am coming with you and bringing the rifle. You won't change *my* mind on that."

…

On Monday they trekked across the fields and through the fence to the Wright farm. As they stepped into the woods and saw the uneven ground, home to so many buried secrets, they were both quiet; it felt like hallowed ground. Cole clasped Belinda's hand and said, "You're the bravest person I know, Blue."

She shook her head, protesting the compliment, and walked out of the thicket toward the small farmhouse. Even from the outside, it looked disorderly. A few wood shingles had fallen and lay in the path to the front door. The unpainted natural wood façade was deep brown, aged over the more than thirty years since it was built. Farming tools were left out in the elements and were rusted and partially covered with soil, showing no use since before the recent rains. Two dirty windows stared at them from either side of a wood door that had a latch instead of a handle.

They turned to look out at the fields. Half of the wheat had not been harvested yet. The corn stood tall and would be ready for harvest within weeks. Weeds had overtaken the vegetable garden.

They turned back to the house. Cole stood about ten feet back to have a clear view in case Tommy should emerge. His hands were positioned on the rifle, ready to raise it if needed. Belinda knocked and stepped back. Alice opened the door and waved them in. It was clear Tommy was not home.

If the exterior had warned them of the disarray in the household, the warning had not been strong enough. The house looked as if a tornado had blown through the indoors. Dirty dishes sat out attracting bugs. Clothes were strewn on the floor and the house smelled of old milk. Belinda looked in horror at the conditions her family was living in. She reflected that she had not entered here since Daddy had died. Had her father actually held things together more than she realized before, or had her mother simply given up after losing him and then Tommy? Then it dawned on her that she was the missing piece. She always cleaned up after meals; she did the laundry and straightened up the house each night.

Belinda saw her mother seated at the table, covered in a scatter of papers, her eyes glazed and vacant. "Mama," she said softly as if to wake her from sleep, but there was no reaction. "Mama.", louder this time, and her mother startled and glanced up.

"Oh, hello, dear." She managed a faint smile as if she were acting out a rehearsed response.

"Mama, what is happening here? Where is Tommy? Why does this place look …" Belinda saw her mother glaze over by the third question and realized she needed to simplify. "Mama. What's wrong?"

"It's all gone wrong, hasn't it now?" It was a statement and not a question.

"Tell me."

"Emit, Tommy, you. It's all over." She paused with her lower lip shaking and tears welling in her eyes. "I'm sorry I didn't protect you."

"Don't worry about that right now, Mama. Let's figure out what we need to do."

"Do? Do?" Her voice raised with the second repetition. "There's nothin' we can do. Emit had more demons than drink; more demons than I even knew. He gambled our lives away. Now Tommy's gone and he ain't comin' back. There's no way out."

"What are you saying, Mama? How did Daddy gamble away our lives?"

"He lost so much. Cards, dice. Always thought he'd be lucky the next time, I guess. He built a debt, then took a note against the farm to pay that debt, plus a little more to win it back next time. He did it 'til he couldn't borrow anymore and the bank shut him down." Her hand drifted to a piece of paper on the table. It was a bank letter threatening to take the land, which was collateral on the note. The amount owed was four hundred dollars, with fifty dollars owed each year at minimum and forty dollars accrued in interest annually.

Belinda felt dizzy and stepped back, bracing against the wall. Cole held her arm. She looked toward no one in particular and spoke in a soft, foggy voice, as if to herself. "It's so much money, and the farm is not even working. We can't pay it. We'll be thrown out. No land. No home. No way to live." Her voice trailed off and she shook her head as tears came.

Alice burst out crying and Buck followed, as if each younger sibling had tied any hope to the next one. As each one gave into despair, the next followed.

Cole was overwhelmed by the despair in the room and his mind cast about for a solution. None came, but he started to speak and found himself showing more confidence than he felt. "We can solve this. You are not going to lose the farm. No one is leaving." They all stared at him, and he could see the faintest glimmer of hope in their eyes, mixed with a greater portion of doubt. Feeling he had to push further, he added, "I promise you."

The walk back to the Thomas farmhouse was quiet. They had gathered up the papers from the table. Cole was deep in thought, racing through figures, calculating yields for different crops, available labor in the small family, bank interest, and costs to feed the family. Every equation equaled a negative number.

They arrived at the farmhouse, scurried inside, and put the papers on the table. Cole turned to Belinda and held her hands. "I meant what I said, Blue. I promise we will figure this out, me and you. We're gonna sit here until we find a way."

She smiled through glassy eyes. "I believe you." She paused. "What if that were our home." He gazed back at her, and she saw the moment he comprehended.

Cole said, "That's it."

Belinda looked cautiously at him. "That's what? It doesn't solve the problem of the banknote."

"No, I mean that's what is supposed to happen. Everything happens for a reason, and we are supposed to buy out that farm and live our lives there." He was talking fast, and his hands moved at a furious pace. "I wanted to move from Ma's farm because I know Dale and Katherine will take it over someday and raise their family here. You want to help raise Alice and Buck. This is why it all happened. The banknote, Tommy leaving ..."

"But I don't see how we pay off the note or make enough to survive," Belinda said, looking cautiously hopeful but concerned.

"Me neither," Cole replied, then paused and flashed a smile that was more confident than he felt, "At least not yet."

They started running through numbers and scenarios, each coming up with ideas that betrayed their flaws before even being fully explained. After a few hours of rehashing facts and figures, Cole was frustrated. No math had worked yet that would save the farm and allow them to pursue their dream as a couple. "OK, one more time ... we've got eight acres to farm. Wheat will yield thirty bushels per acre at about one dollar each, or thirty dollars per acre each year. Corn will get us twenty-six bushels per acre at thirty-five cents per bushel. That's about nine dollars per acre each year. The wheat would get us enough money, but even with me, Ma, and Dale we can only manage three acres with the extra work it takes to bring in a wheat harvest. We'd have to hire a farmhand at eleven dollars per month, plus room and board, and that would eat up all the extra profit. Corn is easy to plant and maintain but barely pays the note."

Shaking her head, Belinda said, "With two acres of wheat and six corn we can make one hundred and four dollars, and fifty will go straight to the bank. That's not including what we eat ourselves. Even if we could survive on fifty dollars a year for five people on the farm, we wouldn't get ahead with almost all of the bank payment going to interest."

Cole nodded. "We'll need to grow more vegetables to feed ourselves. We can rotate crops to some of the higher yields over time. But we have to get rid of that banknote. That's the key to it all."

"Maybe we'll strike gold out in the field?" Belinda said with a laugh and placed her hand on Cole's shoulder to encourage him to keep thinking.

Cole picked his head up as if struck with inspiration. "That's the other piece." He put his hands to the side of his head and grasped at his own hair. "Do you see what's happened in the past few days, Blue? Joseph Mills was telling tales about gold on the day you decided we'd go to town. Kathleen had her baby girl right when you and I were going to … um … try to make one of our own." He smiled sheepishly at Belinda. "Your farm and family are in trouble. Our future is in front of us." He rocked back on the stool. "I need to go west for gold and save your farm … our farm. Twenty ounces would pay the note."

Belinda's head spun for the second time today. She said sharply, "Cole, leaving us, leaving me, can't be the answer."

He leaned over the table, staring into the distance. "I don't see another path. You and I will bring in the rest of the wheat harvest before I go. That should get us close to fifty dollars for the banknote. You and your sister can take in the corn next month and replant and weed the vegetable garden. That'll give you enough to just get by 'til spring, then you'll only plant corn on all eight acres, so you, Alice, and Buck can manage it. You won't make any progress on the debt, but you can survive." He shifted his stool closer to her, sitting face-to-face with her, and reached out to hold both of her shoulders gently. "If you see another way, tell me ..." He paused. "… And if you tell me not to go, I won't."

She looked into his dark eyes, so full of soul, purpose, and belief. Then she thought of Alice and Buck, and even her broken mother. She folded her arms and asked, coolly but with resignation. "How long would you be gone?"

"I'd hope for just over a year if I go fast and make it out there and back in four months each. Of course, I don't know anything about finding gold yet, but I know who to talk to."

"You promise to come back?" Belinda's voice cracked asking the question, her eyes filling with tears.

"I do."

His two words struck her, and she thought he likely intended it to sound like a marriage promise. So, she responded, "We are married in all the ways that matter, you know."

"I know." He smiled, kissed her forehead, and held her close.

…

Cole walked out the front door and saw Ma sitting on the steps next to the post that Tommy had kicked. Tusk sat by her and leaned his head in while she gently stroked his ears. Cole went to speak, but before he could utter a word, she said, "You can use Little Boy, if you think this is the only way." Little Boy was their cart horse, a smaller mount but sturdy and only about five years old. "You should take the dog for company, and some manner of protection."

Ma must have heard through the window. Cole looked at her, staring forward, stone-faced, and knew she was hurting. Ma loved her boys fiercely and it hurt her to see one leave, but she was going to help him anyway. He sat down and kissed the top of her head. "I love you, Ma, and I'll be back."

"Well, you ain't leavin' for a few weeks, as you get that wheat in at Wright farm, so I need to fatten you up a bit before then." She brushed a tear aside quickly and went back inside.

…

That evening after supper, Cole found himself standing in front of the Mills's farmhouse with Tusk by his side. He could barely recall how he'd got there, as he was so deep in thought through the whole walk from his farm. The crickets chirped steadily, and a blanket of stars had swept overhead that he just noticed now. It struck him that each farm looked and felt much the same. If he'd been placed in this spot without knowing where he was, he might have mistaken it for home.

The whitewashed farmhouse, with a barn out back, a vegetable garden, pasture for the horses, and fields of corn and wheat. While it looked and sounded the same as home, Cole didn't see it as mundane. He saw beauty. He thought to himself, *This is a home.* And he felt a pang of loss, knowing he would be headed away from his home soon. He didn't relish the adventure ahead. He dreaded being so far from home, from Ma, from Dale, Katherine, and Eleanor … and most of all, from his Blue.

Joseph opened the front door. "Hey there, you're Dale's little brother, Cole, right?" Joseph was a friendly sort, with bright light brown eyes, dark hair, and a full face. He was stocky, with his shoulders, waist, and hips all close in size so Cole thought he looked a bit like an icebox.

"That's right. Sorry to bother you."

"No bother. What can I do for you?"

"I plan to head west to look for gold." As the words came out, Cole felt he sounded childish and that he had not communicated the full weight of his ambition in such a basic statement, but Joseph didn't seem to notice.

"Well, I can tell you a thing or two about that," Joseph said with a smile.

"That's what I was hoping. I want to learn everything I can from you, so I can get there and get home as safe and as fast as possible."

"Take a seat then." The two of them sat on the front steps. Cole immediately liked Joseph. It felt like they were already friends, though they had only seen each other here and there. "First, let me tell you what not to do. It's a long list, mind you. First, don't plan to go to California. I found gold there, but it's overrun by now. Shoot for Oregon; a lot less people there so far, and I suspect just as good a chance to find gold. I met a few folks on the road back who were headed there. They'd gotten good reports from others. If you leave soon, you might still be in the early groups headed there."

He took a deep breath and kept on. "Second, when you find gold, don't tell nobody—I'm sayin' 'when' to be positive, but it's really 'if,' cuz it ain't a sure thing. There're a lot of thieves and bandits out there looking for gold and trouble. They will kill you for it. Third, don't do what I did, bringing it back here. It was a dumb risk I took, being on the road that long with it. Money's easier to hide. Cash out at a refinery. They won't cheat you like business folks and gold buyers will."

He put a hand to his forehead and said, "Shoot, I started in the middle. I suppose you have to get there before you look for gold." He laughed heartily and started with his list again. "Stay to the main path west. I've got a map I'll let you copy down. Travel with groups whenever you can, especially after you pass Missouri and get into the western territories; it'll be safer. The streams are good for fish, and you can trap or shoot rabbits and squirrels along the way. Forget big game, cuz you can't carry 'em."

Cole was transfixed, taking in every detail he could from Joseph's experience. They talked for three hours. Cole asked question after question and Joseph gleefully answered, clearly basking in Cole's admiration. When it came to talk of panning for gold flakes in streams, Joseph retrieved his gold pan from the barn and demonstrated with water from the well.

When Cole finally was ready to leave, with his copied map and head full of new wisdom, Joseph shook Cole's hand, and with a wink, he said, "One more for my list of what not to do. Watch out for the whores. You'll catch somethin' nasty."

"No chance of that," Cole said with a laugh. "This means a lot. I can't thank you enough."

Joseph handed Cole his gold pan and a small pickaxe, wished him luck, and they parted.

…

While the walk to the Mills's farm was a blur to Cole, the walk home was vivid. His senses were alive, and he took note of everything. The moon was a few days past full and hung low in the sky, almost egg-shaped and throwing off a steely white light that shone through the leaves of the full August trees. The light made a pattern through the trees like a loosely woven cloth stretched out over the sky. An owl hooted, which elicited a low growl from Tusk. Cole's boots scuffed along the dirt road which sounded like Ma's broom on their wood-plank floors.

A willow tree by the left side of the road ahead draped out over the road, catching moonlight between its densely layered, cascading branches. It reminded him of Belinda's hair. He walked through Cold Spring, which was deserted and silent. The general store was dark, and the feed store, which would be bustling with carts during the day, sat stark and empty. It felt as if he'd already left town and was just looking back at it from afar.

Cole arrived back at the farm and stopped to look at his home. He realized he was crying and wondered how far back in his walk he had started. The weathervane creaked softly as a mild wind turned it. It was pointed west.

September 1950 – Cold Spring, New York

The wheat on the Wright's farm was weedy and poorly tended, but with work, they harvested forty-five bushels. At one dollar per bushel, plus a little money they already had, they were able to pay the banknote for the year. The corn harvest would need to feed the family and provide enough money for the winter.

Cole and Belinda worked mostly in silence as they cleaned up the Wright's farm and prepared for his journey to come. They made small talk and spent time together, but the time was more waiting than anything.

On the first Sunday of September, Ma had everyone over for dinner. Cole was set to leave in the morning. He had packed his rucksack, planned his route, based on Joseph Mills' map, and stowed away what meager savings he had to bring. Dale and Katherine were there with little Eleanore, and all the Wrights came too, even Belinda's mother, who looked somewhat more herself since Belinda had been helping restore order to the house.

The meal was beef and potatoes, the usual Sunday supper. When supper was over, Ma brought out her Rhubarb pie, Cole's favorite. She moved like a hummingbird all night, serving food and refreshing the water in everyone's cups, looking as if she felt she would collapse if she stopped moving.

The Wrights headed home, and then Dale and Katherine took Eleanor to go. Dale turned and came back in, threw his arms around Cole, held him tight, and said, "Good luck, little brother." He quickly turned and walked out, and Cole wondered if Dale may have even teared up. He could not remember the last time they had hugged.

Ma waved Cole into the kitchen and put her arms around his midsection, squeezing him tightly. She started to let go reluctantly a few times, each time reestablishing her hold for a bit longer. After several minutes she took a small pouch from her apron pocket and placed it in his hands. It was a portion of her savings and Cole started to object. He knew how much she needed her money, especially with him leaving the farm and reducing their workforce, but he met her eye and realized two things immediately; he would not win the objection and it would only serve to hurt his mother's feelings. So, he nodded and smiled in thanks and hugged her long and hard again.

Ma wiped a tear, cleared her throat and said, loud enough for Belinda to hear in the other room, "I'll see you kids in the morning. Belinda, I need my sleep, so why don't you go ahead and stay with Cole." It was her gift to them. She knew the pain of losing a lover.

They walked into Cole's bedroom, undressed in silence, and laid together, naked, wrapped up with each other so tightly it was hard to distinguish their bodies from each other. They held tight, afraid to let go, neither of them loosening their grip. Cole could not say if an hour passed or two before he fell asleep, but he woke during the night, and they had not let go of each other still. The moonlight streamed in through the window highlighting Belinda's hair, draped over a naked shoulder. Cole looked at her, marveling at the sheer beauty before him, wondering if he could really leave in the morning.

Daylight came into the room and Cole woke. He kissed Belinda's mouth, and she responded in her half-sleep. They kissed gently over and over, neither wanting to break from this moment. "Blue, if you ask me to stay, I will."

Belinda looked into his dark eyes and was tempted to say the word *stay*. It would be so easy, and this pain would go away. But she thought of Alice and Buck. Their daddy was dead, and their big brother had left. However flawed those men were, it hurt those kids that they were gone. Their mother was a broken woman, and the family debt would sentence them to a life of poverty. Neither she nor Cole, had come to another solution that would save Alice and Buck. She said nothing back to Cole and just kissed him again.

…

Ma made a hearty breakfast, even giving Tusk a full portion of bacon and eggs as if he were sitting at the table. She packed a few days' worth of food for Cole. She stood before him glassy-eyed and said, "Just come back in one piece, you hear?"

"I will, Ma." Cole pulled her into his arms and hugged her tightly. He felt a small quake in her as she fought back tears. She was a large figure to him but felt small now as he rested his head atop hers. "You are the best mother anyone could have. I love you, Ma."

Cole put the food Ma had packed for him into his rucksack and slung it over his shoulder. He went outside where Little Boy was lashed to the stair railing. He noticed the cracked wood. It seemed so long ago that Tommy had kicked and broken it; after Ma had stared him down at gunpoint. Cole felt older, though only months had passed. The memory of Tommy felt less scary now, but perhaps that was only because he wasn't around anymore.

His chest pounded when he looked at Belinda. Leaving her was harder than anything he had ever done. The journey did not scare him, and neither did the thought of bandits, wolves, or other dangers. He was afraid of being without his Blue. He had not spent more than a day away from her since he was eleven years old. Even when she had measles, he snuck over to her house, against Ma's orders, and sat outside her window and talked with her. Now, he was about to spend at least a year, and likely more, without her.

They looked at each other and knew the same thoughts were running through their heads. Belinda kissed him and ran into the house. She could not stand to watch him leave and he was not sure he could go through with leaving if she were there.

Cole rode at a walking pace out to the road, with Tusk walking by Little Boy's side. In a moment, he was out of view.

October 1850 – New York and Pennsylvania

"The first mile is the hardest," Cole told himself. He had about three thousand miles to travel on the route he had plotted. The first part of the journey would take him halfway across the country on the same route Joseph Mills had traveled, to Independence, Missouri. From there he would travel a path Joseph told him about that the western settlers had been using for about twenty years that stretched up into the Oregon Territory. It was a longer route than cutting straight across the northern states and territories, but it would be worth the extra distance to stay a little warmer in the coming winter months.

At twenty-five miles each day, he could be in gold country sometime in January, if everything went perfectly, though he knew that was not likely to be the case. Joseph and he had reasoned that fewer prospectors, and fewer bandits and outlaws, would be headed to Oregon over winter. The moving streams didn't ice over and could be panned. Joseph had also heard that the Northwest didn't get as cold as New York—"It's something with the warmth of the Pacific Ocean," he had said.

These thoughts raced through Cole's mind, and then he smiled to himself and thought, "Mile two."

Cole slid down off of Little Boy and walked, leading the horse. With Tusk along, and needing distance more than speed, he had decided all three would walk most of the time. The horse was loaded up with packs of supplies for their trip, but he had packed light with no more than fifty pounds for the horse to carry. Three miles each hour and nine hours of walking each day would keep him ahead of pace and allow for the occasional slow day.

It was only three hours until Cole realized he was traveling where he never had before. The wider roads near Cold Spring had narrowed now to paths that could accommodate a single cart. It was a jarring reminder of how big the world was and how small he was in it. He was setting out for at least four months of travel in one direction, but in three hours he'd gone farther than he ever had before. He reached down and patted Tusk as they walked. "I hope you picked the right man to join up with, boy."

As the sun centered overhead, the three travelers stopped for some food. Cole located a place where Little Boy could graze and there was a stream close enough for them all to drink water. It was cooler today than it had been all last week. A thin layer of cloud cover veiled the full force of the sun but allowed it to peer through, like looking at a candle glowing behind white curtains. He unpacked some of the meat from breakfast and a crust of bread, sharing both with Tusk. He would eat the fresh foods Ma packed for him over the first few days and then move to smoked meats that would keep longer. He hoped to make it all last as long as possible by netting fish or snaring rabbits and squirrels along the way. The longer he kept a food store, staying a few days ahead on food supply, before living meal to meal, the better.

The travelers gathered up and set out hiking again after about fifteen minutes. Cole was not one to sit still and it seemed his companions were up to the task. Little Boy was a young horse and walked ably. Tusk was perhaps seven or eight years old by Cole's estimation, if he had been about a one-year pup when they found each other, so he was not a young dog, but he trotted along with ease, occasionally running ahead and then waiting.

As the afternoon wore on, the path widened and became a small road. Farms reappeared, speckling the hilly countryside. Familiar scents filled Cole's nostrils: wheat, manure, farm air. The road curved slightly to the left and downhill, revealing a town center ahead. They walked through without stopping. No provisions were needed only fifteen miles or so into their journey. Two boys sat in front of the general store and stared at the three travelers. New people were rare in any of these small towns and bore close inspection.

Cole nodded and said, "Hello, boys." Then he laughed to himself recalling his walk to town with Belinda and being mistaken for two boys on the way and later as two girls. He briefly questioned himself as to whether those were actually both boys he had just seen. He laughed again but also felt a grip of sadness in his chest, missing Belinda, and a tear escaped his eye.

At dusk, Cole decided to make camp, while he had enough light to set his snares and fishnet. He figured he had covered more than twenty-five miles, a good day with no difficulties. It gave him confidence for the months to come, though he knew he was in the very first steps of a long journey with unpredictable times ahead. The weather was ideal, with a cooler night breeze blowing and no sign of rain. He decided to leave his burlap cover packed and sleep out in the air tonight. He had painstakingly coated the burlap with pine tar to resist water. He knew there would come days and nights when staying dry would be his primary concern.

He took the saddle and packs off of Little Boy and let him wander in the grass while he set up camp. Little Boy could be trusted not to wander far, but he would tether him with a long rope overnight. He removed the fishnet first. His father had taught him how to tie a net when he was seven. He'd made this one with him. He smiled, recalling how proud he was. The net was made of sturdy, narrow twine laid in perpendicular rows and tied at one-inch lengths where each strand crossed another. The result was a loose net with one-inch squares between the threads of twine. It allowed water and small fish to flow through easily while holding any fish bigger than an inch top to bottom. A thread of twine ran through the top and could be pulled tight to make a basket shape.

Cole brought the net to the edge of the stream that ran about fifty yards down a slope to the right of the path. It was about fifteen feet wide and no more than a foot deep. The water moved quickly through the gentle bend in the stream where he stood. He pulled the twine through the top to make the circular opening to the net about six inches across. He placed the net in the water where there was a natural flow between two rocks, then used a rock to drive two sticks deep into the riverbed and fastened the twine to it. The result was the opening in the net sat between the two rocks and the basket-shaped net bottom was downstream of the opening. He then took a length of twine and tied it through the top of the net and to a tree root at the edge of the stream. He knew that the sticks he drove into the bed could hold the net against the flowing water but would give way to a fish struggling to break free, then the opening would cinch shut trapping the fish.

Satisfied with his net, he went to set up snares. First, he looked for small tracks or patches in the pine needle floor of the wooded area between the path and the stream. He fashioned a loop of twine and found a few good, strong branches to break off as stakes. Pounding the stakes into the ground, he tied off one end firmly and looped the other end of his slipknot loop loosely over the other stake. He repeated this process in four places. He took out more of the food Ma had packed and made a meal for himself and Tusk, then brought Little Boy down to the water.

The good weather allowed him to go with no fire. He settled in with his rucksack as a makeshift pillow and closed his eyes. Tusk curled up next to him. The buzz of crickets, after a long day of walking, lulled him into a sleep, and he stayed that way until just before dawn. He stood and stretched. Tusk looked up as if begging for a few more minutes of sleep but followed Cole's lead, first standing, then stretching. They walked down the slope toward the stream and Cole gave Little Boy a pat on his way by. He collected the empty snares along the way, which made Cole worry about food supplies. Reaching the edge of the stream, he dipped low and drank, with Tusk following suit.

Looking up he could see that the net had broken loose from the stakes pounded into the streambed. It was three or four feet beyond where he placed it, held by the twine tied to the tree root. It was a good sign, but he feared that perhaps a branch may have caught in the net. Wading closer he could see movement in the net, he had a fish. His pride outweighed his excitement for the food itself. This was a sign he was capable of making this journey.

Cole pulled the net from the water and saw a nicely plump brown trout wiggling inside. He removed a small blade knife from a sheath on his belt and filleted the fish right there on the shore. He would need a fire now after all. Cole hiked up the slope as Tusk cleaned up the remains of the gutted fish. He retrieved his flint and gathered kindling to start his fire.

The fish made for a hearty breakfast and allowed for Tusk to have a serving too. The light was just becoming full, and they were ready to break camp and start day two. "Day two," Cole said to his animal companions. "You boys just don't know how long we'll be going. Then again, maybe I don't know all that much either."

...

The first week went quickly and smoothly. Cole tried to tell himself that it would not be this easy, that challenging times would come, but it was difficult not to become overconfident. On only one day had he failed to catch a fish or snare a rabbit or squirrel, so there was meat each day and he had not dipped into the smoked meats from home yet. He rode Little Boy only an hour or two each day, opting to walk and preserve his horse's strength. The weather had been perfect for travel and his two companions seemed in high spirits. By Cole's account, they were ahead of pace, building up a few extra miles each day that would come in handy when the weather turned.

Some days they saw few or even no other travelers. On other days they would see the telltale signs of a town, with the path widening to a road and they would see farmers bringing goods to market or just walking to town for provisions. Cole reflected that Western New York State looked and felt a lot like the Hudson Valley.

It was just after noontime on day nine, and they had just gotten back on the road after a short rest with food and water when Cole heard thunder in the distance. Little Boy skittered sideways a step, but Cole urged him on. The wind picked up and blew large bows on trees back and forth several feet. He could see the treetops ahead swaying like men having had too much drink. Minutes later, the clouds burst, and large drops pelted the travelers.

Urged on by Cole, the trio marched forward. He did not want to give up a full half day's progress, though he knew they would need to shelter soon. Two hours into the driving rain, they were soaked through. Tusk gave a pathetic look up at Cole as if to ask why they were out in this storm. The sky had gone blank, and the underside of the billowing storm clouds looked like water boiling in a black cauldron. A crack of lightning lit the sky. It felt near and Cole guided his companions into a thicket of trees.

He removed his burlap cover from the bag on Little Boy and proceeded to tie a line between branches and sling the rain cover over it. He then tied off each corner, stretched it wide, and staked it to the ground, using a rock to drive branch shards into the wet soil. By the time he looked up at his work, Tusk already sat in the middle of the newly covered area, looking wet and scraggly but pleased with himself. "Do ya mind if I join you in there, boy?" Cole said with a laugh.

There would be no snares or fishnet today. Cole had to focus on drying out his clothes for the next day's travel. They lost at least ten miles of potential progress today. He gathered pine needles that were under the top layer on the ground and as close to large tree trunks as possible, as they were mostly dry. He then gathered the wood closest to the tent, running out and back in quick bursts. Little Boy was tethered right next to them, but he likely would have stayed even if he were loose. The horse was nervous and sidled close to the tent. Cole spoke to him softly, which seemed to calm him down. It took more effort than usual, but the fire started reluctantly, sputtering but eventually sprouting flames; the heat becoming steady and overwhelming the damp wood. The fire sat at the front edge of the covering, just inside for some protection from the rain, but close enough to the edge to allow the smoke to billow out.

Cole stripped naked and laid his clothes close to the fire. He leaned in for warmth. Tusk laid a few feet back, getting some warmth, but was wary of the flames. The wood crackled and gave off a smoky odor that reminded Cole of sitting by the fire pit with Ma and Dale at the farm. He closed his eyes and drifted in and out of sleep while sitting upright, with his chin nestled in his hands and his elbows propped on his bent knees.

Tusk let out a high-pitched bark that startled Cole awake. There were flames over his head as if he were in the fires of hell and he couldn't comprehend what was happening at first. Little Boy started to whinny and pull at his tether. Cole got his bearings and rolled out from under the burlap cover that was ablaze. A spark from the wet wood had ignited the burlap cover, which had been densely coated in pine pitch. The bottom side was ablaze, but it had not burned through the top yet, which was still being pelted by steady rain. Moments after he and Tusk were out from under the burning tent, the twine holding the center up between two branches burned through, and the makeshift tent collapsed on the ground. Most of the flames went out immediately, smothered between the burlap and the wet ground. Looking at the smoky remains, Cole saw a jagged hole had burned through the top of his tent at the spot where the flames had been smothered.

"How could I have been so stupid?" Cole said out loud to himself and his animals. Pine pitch made an excellent water repellent but also burned readily, which he knew. He also knew that if Tusk had not alerted him, he may have been wrapped in burning pine tar. He had to be smarter, more thoughtful in his actions. Now, he just hoped to salvage most of the burlap cover. That night they slept without protection from the rain, which fell until about midnight, then mercifully relented. In the morning, he recalled his bravado of just two days prior. This was a stark reminder that he had much to learn and the price to pay for mistakes on your own in the woods was high. He was lucky this time but could not hope to be always.

…

The terrain looked the same for the next two weeks. They trekked through wooded paths that followed streams and connected to wider paths or dirt roads as they approached towns. Cole had not noticed when they passed from Western New York State into Northern Pennsylvania but learned his location when he asked an older man with a cart of melons near one of the towns they passed. He began to wonder if all of America looked exactly like Cold Spring.

He had stopped for a few provisions after the fire and purchased a small flap of material and a needle to make repairs to his tent cover. He used a few long, strong hairs from Little Boy's tail as thread and made a suitable repair.

It was late October and the air had turned colder. Late in the afternoon, Cole saw the road widen and he knew they were approaching a town. As he rounded a curve, the road he was on was joined by another and he saw three horse-drawn carts ahead of him, walking up a gentle rise. He reached that rise and the valley beyond was revealed. Cole stood, dumbfounded at what lay before him. Several more carts, horses, and various people were on the hillside below, headed to the largest town he had ever seen. He pulled his crude map out and pointed to Pittsburgh.

The sun was setting behind the city, which made it look as if the buildings were ablaze. Dozens of building-lined streets clustered between the fork of a wide river. Even at a distance, it felt like a bustle of chaos, and yet it was exciting. He could see a bridge that was like no structure he had ever seen. A marvel of engineering to cross such a wide river with stone and timber. He felt a rush of excitement and fear at the scale of the city below. He felt small and unworldly but also captivated. The city below made him realize in an instant that all he had known, to this point in his life, was a fraction of the possibilities and potential in the world.

Cole approached the bridge and marveled. He did not know such a thing could be built by men. It stretched hundreds of feet over the river, supported by large stonework towers that sprung up out of the water every fifty feet or so. The bridge itself was brown, weathered wood and built like a long, low, narrow barn, covered from end to end with a slightly pitched roof, peaked in the center. Standing with a straight-on view, and slightly uphill of the bridge, the peak cut a perfectly straight line over the water as if it were one continuous plank, laid over a small stream. A signpost read "Allegheny River Bridge – 25 cents to cross; Horse and cart 50 cents." A short, chubby man in his forties with long, bushy sideburns but no beard or mustache sat on a stool at the entry to the bridge collecting tolls. A horse and cart passed him after handing him coins, then Cole stepped forward.

The toll collector wore overalls and a blue knit overcoat. His face was red from the cool air, and he gave an appraising look at Cole and his animals. He rubbed his chin, as if thinking, and said, "That'll be fifty cents. Twenty-five for you and same for the horse, since you ain't got no cart. I won't charge for the dog."

Cole nodded and wore a look of amazement, stammering, "Thank you. This bridge … how … I mean, uh …"

The man smiled and said, "First time to Pittsburgh, eh?" It was clear he had pride in his city and this bridge. "This bridge was built starting in 1819 and more'n thirty years hence, she's still a beauty, ain't she?"

"I've never seen anything like it." Cole fished out coins to pay the toll and handed them over. "Thank you, sir," he spoke, not looking at the man and sounding far away.

"That's how I felt when I first saw it too when I was about your age." The man smiled, then grabbed Cole's arm gently and pulled him back as he started to cross. "You seem like a nice kid and you ain't been to the city. Watch yourself; there's some bad folk who'll spot a country kid quick and try to take what's yours."

Another horse-drawn cart pulled up to the bridge. Cole thanked the toll man and stepped onto the first planks with Little Boy walking behind and Tusk at his side. The sound of their steps on the wood planks below echoed in the low rafters above them, making it sound like an army of men and horses. As they approached the Western end of the bridge, the low sunset streamed in. The opening grew as they got nearer, revealing the sights and sounds of a bustling city.

Exiting the bridge, he was met immediately by a man, who put an arm on his shoulder and said, "Hello, friend, and welcome to my city. I can see you ain't from here, so it's a good thing you found me. I know where to set you up to stay and the best places for drinks, cards, and girls. The name's Billy and I just like takin' care of visitors to our fine city."

Cole looked stunned and stayed silent a moment. The man was tall and lean, stood with a slight hunch, and tilted his head to the right as he talked. He had yellow teeth and greasy hair and gave off an odor that made Cole think of Emit Wright. Thinking back to the toll man's warning, Cole said, "I'm just passing through, but thank you kindly, Billy."

Undeterred, Billy pressed on. "Well, you surely need to at least stay the night. Let me set you up, my friend. Just follow me this way, and …"

Cole cut in, his instincts telling him he had to be firm, "No, sir. I'll make my way. Goodbye." He felt harsh. He was not used to having to be coarse or abrupt, but he suspected this would not be the last time.

Billy grumbled, "Suit yourself, country boy."

Joseph had told Cole about a place he stayed in Pittsburgh and Cole had written the name on the back of his crude map—The Old Stone Tavern. This would be his first time sleeping indoors for more than three weeks and he looked forward to it. He walked down the main street that ran in line with the end of the bridge and marveled at the number and size of the buildings, packed together like cornstalks in their field back home. The closest together he'd seen buildings before was in Cold Spring where there were only about one hundred feet between the general store and the feed store. Here, some of the buildings bumped right against each other, some had alleys between them not ten feet wide. He glanced down the alley between two buildings and saw a woman on her knees sucking on a man, who held her head with both hands. He looked away quickly.

The street was bursting with activity. People walked their horses; horse-drawn carts and carriages rolled by; drunkards staggered to and fro. Cole felt he'd entered another world. A day prior he wondered if all of America looked like Cold Spring, now he knew there were bigger, stranger places. A woman called out to him, "Hey, handsome, wanna have some fun?" He looked up to see several women standing in front of a two-story wooden building, painted red, with small windows on the second floor.

"No thank you, ma'am," he replied and dropped his head. He heard all of women burst out in laughter at his response. He looked down at Tusk and saw the same wide-eyed expression that he imagined was on his own face, and said to his dog, "I guess you haven't seen a place like this either, huh, boy?"

At the end of the block, he saw a sign hanging, slightly askew, that read "Old Stone Tavern – Est. 1782." He tethered Little Boy to a post out front, pulled down his rucksack, and turned to go inside. Tusk followed. "I'm not sure you can go in there, boy." Cole reached into his sack and broke a small strip of smoked pork off. He tossed it near Little Boy, and Tusk chased it down and chewed it eagerly. "You stay here, boy."

The tavern was a large rectangular building, two stories, with a row of five evenly placed windows across the second floor. Two doors faced the front on the bottom floor, each with a sign over the top of the frame; one read Inn and the other Tavern. As he entered the door to the inn, he saw a small office and reception desk to his left and an opening in the wall to his right where he could see into the tavern that was in full swing already in the early evening.

A man at the counter to the left asked, "Will you be needing accommodations?" He wore a smock over a denim shirt. He was in his fifties and had gray hair, thinning on top, and a full face cleanly shaven. He looked curiously at Cole, who was almost eighteen but looked younger.

"Yes, sir, and I have a horse and a dog."

"We can put you in a nice room upstairs and stable your horse out back. The dog can stay in the pen with your horse. It's seventy-five cents for the room and we'll give you breakfast. Another twenty-five cents for the stable and my stable boy will clean up your horse. My name's Bo. Ask for me if you need anything."

Cole brought Little Boy around back and removed his rucksack with his money and extra clothes. He left the other supplies with the horse and handed the lead to the stable boy, who was not more than ten years old and had reddish-brown hair to his shoulders and a dirty face full of freckles. "This is Little Boy. Keep an eye on Tusk as well, please." He motioned to the dog, who was looking up confused. "Put him in with the horse and close the gate. He's not used to being left behind." He handed the boy ten cents. The boy grinned and gave Tusk a pat, leading him into the stable.

After paying for his room, Cole went upstairs. The room was only barely larger than the narrow bed, which was a simple wood frame with a thin mattress, but it promised the most comfortable night's sleep he had had in close to a month. He threw his sack on the bed and closed the door to head down to the tavern for something to eat and a beer. He paused outside the door, went back in, picked up the rucksack, and took it with him for safekeeping.

The tavern was a carnival of sights and sounds. Patrons sat at stools along the bar, and a handful of tables, each seating four, filled the middle of the room. Against the far wall, a man wearing a white shirt and a dusty brown vest played a piano with a lively beat. To the front, along the windows, a higher, narrow table had individual stools in a row that were empty. Cole ordered a beer and a bowl of stewed beef and took a seat on one of the stools. It gave him the best vantage point to watch the room; he was fascinated by it all.

The stew was room temperature, having likely been cooked hours before, but it tasted fine. A poker game was ongoing at one of the center tables, four men receiving their cards, putting in a penny ante, and then wagering on their hands. Cole had played cards with Dale before, so he knew the basics of what hands beat others. Four of a kind beat three; three of a kind beat two; two pair better than one, and higher cards win when hands are equal otherwise. Dale and Cole played at night in their room when they were younger. Their dad had taught them. They bet with salted sunflower seeds and usually ate the winnings while the game went on. Dale would seem to bet on every hand, but Cole would figure out his chances of winning and bet only when they were good.

The four men playing cards all looked to be in their late twenties. Across the table, facing Cole, was a slim man with a denim shirt and a bowler hat. His long brown hair cascaded from under the hat and around a narrow face that sprouted a scraggly beard. To his left was a plump man with black hair and overalls. He was pushed against the table and part of his belly spilled over the edge of it. The man with his back to Cole was short and stocky. His feet barely touched the floor, dangling from his chair. The last player was a nervous-looking, sandy-haired man with a sharp nose and pursed lips. He reminded Cole of what Emit Wright may have looked like years younger.

The nervous man dealt to the man with the bowler hat and then around the table. He dealt five cards to each and then a round of betting began. When they traded cards in after the bets, Cole knew they were playing five-card draw. It was the game he and Dale played, and he guessed must be the most common poker game in most places. The math of card games always fascinated Cole; thirteen types of cards in four suits made up the fifty-two-card deck. With four men playing, twenty cards were dealt, then up to another twelve dealt in trade, but usually less. He had heard gambling men talk of straights and flushes, or four of a kind or a full house, but when he thought about the math, he suspected he could watch this game all night and not see a single one of any of those hands. In the times he played with Dale, the best he'd seen in five-card draw was three of a kind, and even that was pretty rare.

There was a whoop of joy when the hand ended, and the chubby man reached out to pull the handful of pennies in the pot over to his side of the table. With his belly wedged against the table, he could barely reach the money. The next hand started with the man in the bowler hat dealing. Cole watched the players look at their cards. The chubby man showed a flash of disappointment in his eyes but then smiled broadly to conceal it. The short man faced the other way so Cole could not see a reaction. The nervous man's mouth curled up slightly with the faintest trace of a smile. The bowler hat man showed no reaction.

The first two men passed on betting and then the nervous man threw in five cents. The bowler hat matched but the other two players folded, losing only their penny ante. Cole could see sweat forming on the nervous man's face. He traded only one card. The bowler hat man traded three. He smiled broadly and looked into the eyes of the nervous man, who immediately rechecked his hand.

It was obvious to Cole what was happening. The nervous man had been dealt two pair originally, which is why he only drew one card, hoping to match either pair and make it a full house, but that had not happened. The other explanation for the one-card draw would have been looking for a straight or flush, but he had seen the flash of excitement in the man's face when he looked at the initial deal. He was certain it was two pair. The other hand was harder to tell, but he was fairly sure it was a bluff. The man in the bowler hat showed no reaction at all when looking at his initial hand. The broad smile at his draw was intended for the nervous man to notice. It seemed to be working, based on the growing beads of sweat on the man's brow. He looked as if he might get sick and vomit right on the table.

The nervous man bet twenty cents and did his best to look confident. The man in the bowler gave a sly grin, like a man who just trapped prey and was going in for the kill. He pulled a dollar out and raised the bet. The nervous man slumped his shoulders and shook his head. He looked back down at his cards and muttered something Cole could not hear. Cole found himself urging him on under his breath. "You have the winning hand, don't let him bully you." But the silent urgings failed.

He threw his cards down, face up, and yelled, "God dammit! I had sixes and nines. Best hand I had all night." The man in the bowler hat placed his cards face down, gathered up the rest of the cards, passed them left, and then swept up his winnings. The nervous man looked incredulous and shot a look at the winner. "You ain't even gonna show me what you had? Well, shit." There was no reply.

Cole watched the game for the next hour, fascinated by the interplay between these men. He felt like he had joined their group, secretly. He had a name for each, Bowler, Chunk, Shorty, and Sweaty. He knew some of those were unkind, but it was only in his head, and he would not speak them. He could guess the type of hand Chunk and Sweaty had almost every time. Bowler was too even-tempered and expressionless to know, and Shorty had his back to him. He did figure out Shorty's hand a few times just based on learning when and how he bet.

What sounded like a child's voice came to Cole's ear, and he turned to see a young woman wearing a low-cut dress showing most of her breasts. She had curly dark hair that fell onto her bare shoulders. Her face had pale, milky skin with heavy red coloring rubbed into her cheeks and painted red lips. Cole had never seen makeup like this and he immediately did not like it.

She looked more like a painting of a woman than an actual one to him. Her green eyes below her dark eyebrows were striking but appeared sad and distant.

She spoke again in a high, childlike voice. "Hi, you can call me Missy. You passin' through?"

"Yes, I'm headed to Missouri." Cole had heeded another one of Joseph Mills's cautions; never tell anyone your full plans.

Missy tossed her hair and leaned forward to show her breasts off. "You want some company?"

"The seat's open I think," Cole said politely, motioning to the stool next to him. He saw in her expression that he had missed the point as she cocked her head to the side in a way of checking if he understood her.

After a quiet, awkward moment, she put a hand on Cole's chest, leaned closer, and whispered, "It's a dollar for anything you want. For half, I'll suck you off, and if you only got a quarter, I'll use my hand."

Cole swallowed and studied her face. She was younger than he was and would be pretty without all the paint on her face. "I've got a girl … sorry."

"So do most of 'em," she said with a grin, motioning with her hand to reference all of the men in the room. "But it don't stop 'em." She paused, looking at him. "You're a long way from home, ain't you? There ain't nothin' wrong with a little company far from home."

She looked desperately at Cole, and he felt for her. She looked perhaps fifteen or sixteen years old, and this is what she did night after night. How long had she been here doing this?

He took her wrist gently, removed her hand from his chest, and asked, "What's your name?"

"I told you already, Missy," she said, looking slightly confused, either because he hadn't listened or because he didn't want anything from her.

"No, you told me I can call you Missy. You didn't say that was your real name." Cole gave a wry smile.

Her brow creased as she studied him. After a pause, she said, "Priscilla." Her voice sounded different as she said her real name.

Cole leaned back and said, "Well, Priscilla, you are very pretty, and you can sit here with me, and I'll buy you a beer if you want. But I can't … you know … my girl."

She stepped back and said, "I can't make money sittin' and drinkin'," then she turned away. She took two steps and then paused. Turning back toward him, she walked briskly to him and leaned close to his ear. "One of the men at that table you're watching will get up soon and the man with the hat will invite you to play. Don't—they'll cheat you; I seen it a hundred times." She hurried off to talk with a man at the bar.

A few hands later, the short man with his back to Cole stood, waved to his fellow players, and left the tavern. Bowler waved at Cole, "Come join us, friend."

Cole held up both hands in a shrug and said, "I don't play, and besides, I've got no money." The second statement seemed to end their interest more than the first, and they started looking about for another traveler. Cole headed out to check on his animals and then went to his room to rest for the night.

…

It was a brisk but clear morning. Cole ate breakfast, then went to the stable, smuggling an extra portion of bacon from the tavern for Tusk. The animals looked rested and well cared for. The stable boy had brushed out the knots in Little Boy's tail and mane.

Independence, Missouri was his next waypoint, the place where he would turn northwest and follow the trail that had been forged up to the Oregon Territory. It was about eight hundred miles and Cole hoped to arrive in about five weeks' time. It would likely be the next time he slept indoors. He had to keep his money saved for emergencies.

December 1850 – Cold Spring, New York

The Wright farm had been set to order. Belinda realized now that she had been the consistent force that kept that household moving, even back when she was eleven years old and they had first moved in. She suspected that Tommy knew that too and perhaps that was why he hated her. The root of his hatred and violence was something that always troubled her. In some ways, the reason why he hurt her haunted her even more than the physical pain he had inflicted.

Being there for the past months, Belinda learned that it wasn't that her mother didn't care about keeping order in the house; she just couldn't organize herself. She couldn't figure out what needed to be done next, so she froze and did nothing. Now, with Belinda in charge, her mother would contribute and do her assigned tasks, then ask what was to be done next. Alice and Buck had to be held out of school for the first month while they got the farm in order and working again. Belinda felt badly; she desperately wanted them to be educated. She had attended school through age sixteen, the same as Cole, which was several years longer than most children in the Hudson Valley. The demands of farm life caused most families to put their kids to work in the fields by age twelve when they could pull their weight.

The days were long. Belinda would wake the kids early so they could do morning chores with her; feeding the chickens, watering the animals, gathering eggs, and mucking out the barn. She would start Mama on laundry while she made breakfast for everyone.

On Sundays they ate supper at the Thomas farm. Dale, Katherine, and Eleanor would come as well, making it a party, with all eight of them, except for Eleanor, talking together over a meal of beef, potatoes, and vegetables. Belinda had invited them all to supper at the Wright farm, but Mrs. Thomas would always have an excuse as to why she needed to be home. Belinda knew the story of the Learys, and of Ma's pain of losing her best friend, so she stopped asking.

The Sunday night before Christmas, December 22, 1850, the two families were crowded into the Thomas farmhouse's small family room. Elizabeth, Maye, and Belinda had the three stools at the table and Katherine sat in the rocking chair with Eleanore. Dale joined Alice and Buck sitting on the floor with their backs propped against the wall. A small tree sat on the table with homemade decorations, mostly made years prior by Dale and Cole. The room was buzzing with several conversations at once, as was usual. Katherine was telling Belinda a story about Eleanore's latest accomplishment, crawling forward several feet, while Elizabeth was asking Alice and Buck about their schooling. Dale was just listening and looking about. He was often on the periphery of all conversations. Then he said, "I wonder where Cole's at."

The room went quiet, and they all looked at Belinda. They all thought about Cole often. Belinda and Elizabeth rarely thought of anything else but they never spoke about his whereabouts because it was too painful to say it out loud. They knew it was possible he would never return, or he could even be dead at that moment.

After a pause, Belinda said, "I suppose he could be about halfway now if he's making good time." She had copied a version of his map and would look at it, alone at night. "I think he'd have passed Independence, Missouri and be headed Northwest toward the Oregon Territory." She paused and noticed that a tear had escaped her eye, and everyone was looking at her somberly. She mustered a smile, adding, "Just imagine the stories he'll tell here at Christmas next year."

. . .

The evening was coming to a close, and everyone said their good-byes. Dale hugged Belinda tightly, something he had rarely done, and said, "He'll be OK, Sis. Cole's the smartest kid I know." It was the first time he had ever called her *Sis*, and Belinda felt so much joy at the thought of having a big brother who loved her.

On the walk back to the Wright farm, Alice and Buck ran ahead. Belinda and her mother walked silently. They didn't talk much anyway, and never about anything of substance. Still, their relationship was different now, with Daddy and Tommy gone. Belinda knew her mother appreciated her, by the way she looked back at her with admiration while receiving daily assignments.

"Mama?" Belinda started when the children were out of earshot. She paused and stopped walking. Her mother turned to face her, almost as if she anticipated the question that was coming. "Why did Tommy hate me so much; what did I do?"

The lines on Mama's face, already pronounced, seemed to grow deeper. Her mouth curled down at the corners, and she shook her head. After a long pause, she spoke in a quiet, strained voice. "You didn't do anything to deserve it. I think he hated me but took it out on you." She paused and began to cry, adding through sobs, "I'm so sorry I didn't protect you. I'm sorry your daddy didn't … couldn't. I'm sorry for everything." She broke down and bent over with her hands over her face.

Belinda was moved but didn't reach for her mother. She needed answers. "Why did he hate you then?" Her voice was even and gave away no anger nor sympathy.

"Before we moved here, Tommy's real father came back." Maye lowered her hands from her face and peered up at Belinda with her head still tilted down, like a scolded child.

Belinda stood; mouth open; eyes searching her mother's face. She was about to ask but it was obvious now. How could she ever have thought that Tommy was the product of her two diminutive parents? He bore no resemblance to her father at all. The timing and suddenness of the change in Tommy started to make sense.

"I was pregnant and wasn't married," Mama went on. "The boy wanted nothin' to do with me, and my father cast me out. I had nowhere to live, nowhere to go. Emit always liked me in school, I knew. He'd stare at me and then look away if I ever looked over. He never did get up the courage to talk to me though; he was so damned shy." A sad smile came across her face, and she wiped her tears away. "I went to his house and knocked on the door. You never seen a boy more surprised." She let a small laugh escape. "I told him my story out on the porch, and he just listened. Then your daddy turned to me and said, 'We'll be married then.' You know, those might have been the first words he ever said to me." She laughed with new tears trickling down her face. "Yup, he married me while I was five months along with another man's child. Emit was not a perfect man, lord knows, but he was kind to me, and I grew to love him—and he gave me you three kids, which was the best gift I ever got."

She paused again and looked away, the smile leaving her face, replaced by anger. "Tommy's father always knew, and the bastard came to the house drunk one night, probably just to rub it in Emit's face, and he told Tommy. It messed Tommy up good; started breakin' stuff at the house; cursed me out; wouldn't even look at Emit. I don't think he spoke to your daddy even once after that. Emit was always a drinker but it got worse after that." Maye folded her hands, as if in prayer, and looked as if she were pleading. "But I swear the worst of it all was when he started hurting you." I suppose he always prided himself on being the oldest and wanted to take charge. Of course, you were always the one who took control of things, even from a young age. He may have resented you a bit before, but from that day on he had to run you down at any chance. What kind of mother..." Maye's voice trailed off and her wet eyes searched Belinda's.

Belinda wanted to be angry. Her mother had let her be beaten by her brother. She had known why he was so violent and never told her. She had been weak—a mother unwilling, or maybe just unable, to defend her child. She looked at the woman across from her, looking smaller now than ever. She saw pain beyond just weakness. Belinda put her arms around her and said, "It's OK, Mama."

December 1850 –
Independence, Missouri

*I*ndependence was a swirl of people that topped even Pittsburgh. It felt like a crossroads where everything east met everything west. The trail leading to the Oregon Territory had drawn people of all types to the area. Methodist missionaries assembled, looking to head northwest to bring their religion to native people and the growing region, establishing roots in advance of more population growth. Prospectors passed through here seeking gold either in California or, by increasing numbers lately, the Oregon Territory. Families traveled, seeking free land to cultivate and build their farms and find their dreams in a new world.

With the growing number of travelers in town came a growth in crime. Swindlers took advantage of travelers; thieves robbed families; hucksters sold potions for any ailment. The street seemed to be almost like a carnival. Cole arrived in early December and planned to stay a single night, hoping to meet up with travelers headed to Oregon, heeding Joseph Mills' advice to travel in groups wherever he could, once he was out west.

The weeks since Pittsburgh had been mostly solitary, occasionally meeting up with other travelers, either headed west for gold or land. Most were eager to set a common pace so that they enjoyed the safety of a small group. The weather had turned colder with a brisk late fall feel but there had been no snow yet. Cole had been pleased with the pace overall and felt he could reach the Oregon Territory by sometime in the following February.

As Cole strode into town, leading Little Boy, and with Tusk trotting by his size, he sized up the scene. Like Pittsburgh, there was a main road through town, wide and lined with buildings on either side. The inns were obvious, with a row of second-floor windows facing the road and taverns on the first floor. There was a general store, feed supply, a tanner, and a smith lined along the north side of the road to his right. A church stood on the north side after the first group of businesses and had some space to either side, giving room on the east side for a curved walkway up to the arched front doors, and a cemetery on the west side.

Along the south side of the road, to Cole's left, were two inns, a saloon, and a brothel, that ironically stood directly across from the church. *The two centers of worship, right across from each other*, Cole thought to himself as he chuckled out loud. Beyond the church to his right and the brothel to his left were more buildings he had yet to discover. This was a prospering town, full of activity, even in December, well before the spring, when according to some of his fellow travelers along the way from Pittsburgh, the main flow of people gathered to head on the trail to the Oregon Territory.

Horses and carts lined the street. Cole was drawn to a small covered wagon, stopped in the road with the general store on the right and one of the inns on the left. A family of four stood left of the wagon, all dressed in drab, gray cloth. Most likely a religious family, Cole thought to himself. What had drawn his attention was an animated conversation with a man holding a bottle out toward them and speaking excitedly. Cole walked closer, intrigued by the scene.

The man with the bottle wore a top hat and a bright green coat with gold buttons. He appeared well-fed, with an abundant belly that hung over the belt line of his dark blue trousers. He had a bushy, rust-colored mustache and sideburns.

Cole moved close enough to hear the conversation. "My friend, this will cure what ails you. I see the ill in your pale face. These are no times to be traveling the harsh road to the Northwest while being unwell. One sip of this each morning and you'll be cured, I guarantee." The man held the bottle out and bent toward the man in drab gray.

The man in gray was indeed quite pale, perhaps in his late twenties but looking older than that and ill. His stringy black hair accentuated the ghostlike color of his face. He was gaunt, with hollow cheeks and a bony frame, but he stood tall, a full head taller than the pudgy salesman. Next to him was presumably his wife, a plain-looking woman with an average build and a round face; her hair tucked in a bonnet. She stood with her head not quite reaching the shoulder of her husband. In her arms was one of her two children, a girl of maybe two years or less, who looked bored. Her brown hair leaked out of her matching bonnet sending strands cascading over her face. The other child was a boy of perhaps five years, dressed as his father was, in gray pants and coat. He had darker hair than his sister's, though not as black as his father's. One of his front teeth was missing and had not been replaced with the adult tooth yet. He was fidgeting and pulling at his father's sleeve.

As Cole watched the tall man consider the purchase, he saw the pudgy salesman glance past the potential customer to something behind him, then look nervously back at the man. He held the bottle up and started to repeat some of his sales pitch. Cole followed his eyes behind the man and saw a boy of maybe twelve years climbing into the wagon, obviously attempting to be silent. It was clear, the sale was a distraction—they were working together.

Cole stepped forward, feeling for the family, who looked a bit lost in this big town. "Sir," he called to the stout man in the green coat. All five people stopped and stared at him. "Is that your boy in the back of this wagon?"

The man looked stunned and fumbled for words, but none came. The tall man in gray spun around and ran to the back of the wagon.

Cole continued, "I just don't want him to fall and get hurt, that's all."

The tall man pulled the boy from the cart, who then wriggled free and ran off. The family and Cole watched him go, but none felt inclined to give chase. When they turned back, the brightly dressed salesman had gone.

The tall man shook his head then turned to Cole and extended a hand, speaking formally. "My name is Cyrus Ryerson and I owe you my thanks." His voice was soft, with a hint of a wheeze.

"It was no bother. It was obvious what they were up to

from where I stood. I'd hope someone would do the same if it were happening to me." Cole shook his hand and smiled. "I'm Cole and my fellow travelers here are Little Boy and Tusk." He motioned to each animal. Tusk had already started licking the little boy's hand, who was now kneeling beside the dog and rubbing his head.

Cyrus looked to his wife, who nodded and smiled, then he asked, "Would you join us for supper at the tavern, Cole, as our way of showing appreciation?"

Cole had not had more than passing conversations with relative strangers for weeks and welcomed the opportunity to join them.

Smith's Inn was the first building on the left, entering town from the east. They had all agreed to meet at the tavern on the first floor for supper, so Cole decided to seek accommodation there as well. The building looked fairly new, likely built within the past two years as the town expanded out from the church at its center, growing due to the rising number of travelers headed west. This was the start of the trail northwest to the Oregon Territory and it was a thriving community. There were eight small rooms upstairs, barely larger than the beds they held but perfect for passing travelers looking for a night or two of comfort indoors. There was a small stable out back where Cole was able to get Little Boy and Tusk situated.

…

At supper, Cyrus introduced his wife, Phoebe; son, William; and daughter, Charity. All were polite and proper, with even little Charity offering a handshake. It made Cole homesick to see Eleanore and to know how she was growing and what she was learning during her first year. It was possible that he would not see her again until she was almost as old as Charity.

They talked openly as they dined on roast pork and potatoes at the tavern in Smith's Inn. There were only eight tables, with four chairs each, in the tavern. Phoebe held Charity on her lap, while William got his own chair and knelt on it to reach the table. He had a round face and his straight hair hung down in a perfect circle around his head like an upside-down bowl. There was a steady current of conversation around them. When asked what brought him west, Cole gave an abbreviated version of the financial trouble with the Wright's farm, his friend Belinda, and his mission to go to the Oregon Territory in search of gold. He left out any mention of Tommy's violence.

"You must love this Belinda very much." Phoebe smiled, seeing through his description of his 'friend.'

"I do," Cole replied instantly and almost involuntarily. His eyes started to well with tears at the thought of her, so he quickly turned the conversation. "Tell me about your journey."

"We're gonna teach injuns 'bout Jesus," piped up William.

Cyrus smiled and patted Willams head with his long gangly fingers. "That's right, son." Turning to Cole, he became serious. "We are Methodists, and I am a pastor. We're following the great Jason Lee who established a mission in the Oregon Territory, bringing the teachings of Christ to the natives there. He started the mission ten years ago and sadly passed five years back. We aim to continue his teachings and bring more children of God to the light."

"Amen," added Phoebe, eyes closed, hands clasped, and shaking her head side-to-side in the manner Cole had observed women in church who were apparently feeling the holy spirit.

Grasping Cole's arm, Cyrus looked into Cole's eyes and said, "It's the will of God." He let out a wheezy cough and winced after it.

Cole was not sure he believed it was the will of God, but he knew that this family believed it and he liked them instantly. They had a clear purpose and were not going to be deterred. They were like him in that way. Studying the gaunt Cyrus and hearing his cough, he wondered if the family would actually make it all that way, regardless of their purpose and determination. The road west was challenging. Joseph Mills had told him of the many people he saw buried along the way to California. The road to Oregon would be no easier, especially traveling in the winter months before the mass of travelers embarked in spring.

Chewing the last bite of pork, Cole looked at Cyrus and Phoebe and said, "I leave in the morning for the Oregon Territory. Thank you for the meal and the company. I hope you have safe travels and achieve all you want to in Oregon."

Cyrus looked thoughtful for a moment, then responded, "We leave in the morning as well." Phoebe looked at Cyrus with surprise. He went on. "There's safety in numbers and we'd be happy if you traveled along with us." Pausing, he added, "I believe our meeting was God's will."

Cole would be happy for the company but wondered if the family would slow him down. He had a goal to push through the winter and reach Oregon by late February. He didn't believe in the will of God but he did find that things happened for a reason. This family might need him, or perhaps he might need them, so he nodded and said, "I would be happy to have the company and there's no doubt we're safer together. I cover a good twenty-five miles each day, weather permitting, at a walking pace, as I only ride my horse at need." He had posed his statement as a question, or perhaps a challenge.

Cyrus didn't hesitate, patting the table with both hands. "Then it's settled. With the wagon, none of us have to walk. We move at a walking pace as well, so as not to tire Lee, our horse—we named him in honor of the missionary Jason Lee." Cyrus smiled and turned to his wife, who looked worried but also smiled and nodded.

In the morning, they ate breakfast together then gathered outside. The Ryerson family had slept in the wagon outside, which conserved money but also protected their property. Cole brought Little Boy around and was followed by Tusk who had just enjoyed some of Cole's bacon from the tavern.

As they passed through town, a tired-looking woman sat in front of the brothel, apparently on the early morning shift, looking for potential customers. She appraised the obviously religious family in their drab gray clothes and Cole traveling with them and settled back in her seat, not bothering to even wave. They walked to the far end of town and up the road headed west with half of the country between them and their destination.

December 1850 to March 1851 — The Road to the Oregon Territory

The first day held good weather for Cole and the Ryerson family. It was brisk and clear with blue skies. The sun set at four thirty when they had covered only about twenty miles, so they traveled in the dark until about seven before setting camp for the night. During the day, Tusk had alternated between trotting along with Cole and jumping up into the wagon to enjoy being petted and tussled by the children.

As they set camp, Cole realized a benefit of this arrangement he had not considered. He was able to sleep underneath the wooden base of the covered wagon. The Ryersons slept inside the wagon with Cole and Tusk underneath it. While the family had the benefit of warmth from each other and staying inside the wagon, with flaps drawn down over the back and front openings, Cole relied on a fire, burning far enough from the wagon to pose no danger but close enough to give some heat. Tusk also provided warmth, tucked in by Cole's side.

They were up at first light which revealed a wide, flat landscape ahead of them, lit by the sunrise behind. The morning was cold but clear; it would be another good day for traveling. Cole's snares were empty, and they had not camped near enough to water to set the fishing net, but they had supplies from town that would last the week before they had to rely on what they could catch.

As they set to start out, Cyrus walked to the front of the wagon and began to cough, with a high-pitched wheeze underneath the sound. He coughed over and over for more than a minute, doubled over at the waste. Phoebe came to his side and held him up while rubbing his back. It was clear she had seen this before. When the fit ended, Cyrus did not meet Cole's eye and simply climbed to his spot steering the wagon and patted Lee's hind quarter. Phoebe glanced at Cole and then looked away, the worry showing in deep furrows in her brow.

They covered nearly thirty miles on the second day. It felt good to get ahead of the pace on days with clear travel, as they all knew there would be challenging days ahead when they would make less progress. The group sat around a fire that Cole had made larger tonight to provide more heat as they ate. Cyrus suppressed a few coughs and brought up new topics of discussion after each one, clearly trying to avoid the question on Cole's mind. Cole decided to accommodate him and not ask.

The children had become very fond of Tusk, and he was enjoying the attention. At bedtime, he looked up into the wagon, perhaps wanting the attention to continue, or perhaps just to sleep in the covered area, but Cole needed the dog's warmth. After being cold the night before, tonight he used his burlap tent cover, fastening it with twine to the planks under the wagon. He staked the tent narrowly to keep their body heat contained in a smaller space. It made for a much more comfortable sleep.

...

Three weeks had passed since Cole and the Ryerson family had left Independence, Missouri. Cyrus's cough had grown more persistent, and the wheezing was now audible as he breathed normally. Still, they did not discuss it though they talked of other things throughout each day. A bond was forming amongst the travelers, and it certainly felt to Cole that he was meant to be with them.

No other travelers had been evident along their route, and it was apparent to them all that most of the people in Independence those weeks back were headed on the southerly route toward California. The westward travelers bound for the Oregon Territory likely would not arrive in Independence until spring to avoid the cold and snow. There had been one snowstorm during their travels, about a week prior. They traveled less than fifteen miles that day and found cover in a thicket of trees that helped protect the horses while all five people, plus Tusk, took shelter inside the wagon.

The snow remained today, blanketing the ground and lining the bare tree branches. It had not warmed enough for any to melt over the past week. The clean snow ahead of them made it clear that no travelers had passed this way for at least the past week. To the right of the path, Cole's eye landed on a plain wooden cross, made of two stripped branches tied with twine where they crossed. It had been pounded into the ground in front of a rock pile that looked no more than three feet long. Someone lost a child here. Phoebe and Cyrus were looking as well. No one spoke.

Late that afternoon they arrived at a steep slope. A growth of ash trees clustered at the bottom of the hill below them, and they could see water as well. The area was sheltered from the wind and would make an excellent camp for the night. The slope looked too steep for Lee to walk with the wagon tied to him.

Cyrus pulled out a map and spoke, with some effort through his wheezing, "This is Ash Hollow." He coughed and paused. "Fresh water and a good respite, but we'll have to lower the wagon with a rope. The horse can support it from behind but can't walk down with the weight of a wagon behind him.

They untethered Lee from the staves and led him behind the wagon. Cole brought Little Boy to help as well. Cyrus removed some rope from the wagon and began to cough violently. Phoebe took it from him and looped the center of the rope around the rear axle of the wagon. She then brought the two ends out to the back, making sure they were equal in length. She handed one to Cole, saying, "Tie it to the pommel, so it's centered, and we don't get the horses sideways. Then we'll have to lead them down at the same pace. Cyrus will guide the wagon to stay in the center of the path.

Cole looked at her with amazement. This woman had come across as quiet and shy during their three weeks together, deferring to her husband in most matters, but clearly, she was smart and capable. She even looked a bit larger and sturdier to him in that moment.

When everything was in position, they guided the wagon down. William was in charge of walking with Charity ten feet back from the horses and out of harm's way in case the wagon came loose. They reached the bottom without incident and looked around. It felt like a tiny paradise; ash trees rising up around them; water gurgling from a stream into a crystal-clear pool. The water was partly frozen but fully liquid by where the stream entered. Within the small, bowl-shaped valley, the world beyond was invisible and one could imagine nothing else existing. The serenity was marred, though, by three crude crosses, in front of rock piles, just up the southern slope. It appeared to be two adults and one child. Phoebe and Cole stared at the crosses, wondering who they were and what adventure had brought them here. Who had loved them and buried them?

Phoebe grabbed Cole's forearm and said, "If Cyrus ..." She stopped short with tears in her eyes and just shook her head and walked away.

That night they all sat by a fire. Cole's fishnet had secured a bass that they roasted and ate, resetting the net in hopes of fish for breakfast as well. The children went to bed and took Tusk with them into the wagon. Phoebe said, "Tell us about Belinda."

Cole smiled, with the fire's flames reflecting in his dark eyes, he started, "She's the best friend I've ever had ..." And then he told them more than he had ever before, even sharing how Tommy would hurt her and how he had failed to protect her. After a while, he looked up at their faces, almost startled that he'd been talking so freely about things he had not shared with anyone other than Belinda. He realized these people were his friends, perhaps the only other true friends he had ever had.

Phoebe got up to go to bed, saying, "Cole, it's God's miracle to find love like you have." She then kissed the top of Cyrus's head and added, "… like we all have."

When they were alone, Cole looked at Cyrus and asked, "Can I ask you …"

"Diptheria," Cyrus interrupted, without waiting for the full question. "Not a lot the doc could do other than tell me to wait and rest."

Cole looked puzzled. "You aren't exactly resting though. Should you be out here?"

"It's God's plan. I'm called." Cyrus leaned in with a serious look as he spoke through wheezing breaths.

Cole looked incredulous, asking, "How do you know God's plan? Doesn't God want you to live?"

"If I make it there, it's God's plan, just as if I don't."

Cole shook his head, frustrated by this man who he had genuine affection for; a man who had two children to look out for and a wife who adored him. "If rest might cure you …"

"Why are you out here?" Cyrus interrupted.

"I'm doing what I have to …"

"Same as me," Cyrus interrupted again, nodding with a smile.

Cole shook his head. "But it's not God's plan that I'm here. It's just what I have to do, for Belinda and for our future."

"Same thing," Cyrus said, patting Cole's knee. Then he got up, pushing off of Cole to help him stand, and walked to the wagon. He got in and shooed Tusk out.

Cole sat staring at the fire. He heard the sounds of lovemaking from the wagon and fell asleep by the fire with Tusk curled up beside him.

...

Two more weeks went by, and they had passed by dozens of makeshift crosses. They appeared more frequently the farther they traveled west, with some stretches having five or more in a single mile. Cyrus's cough had become constant, and he seemed to have trouble getting enough breath into his lungs. At times he would stagger due to dizziness, but they all pressed on.

Another snowstorm had passed through, leaving nearly a foot of snow but a thaw had reduced it to wet slush that the horses and Cole trod through. Tusk was riding more and more in the wagon. Ahead to the left, they saw a massive rock formation unlike anything Cole had seen in his life. It was perhaps a half mile long and two hundred feet high of sheer rock. Phoebe grabbed the map and called out, "Independence Rock."

As the words came out of her mouth, Cyrus toppled sideways, limp in the wagon seat and then over the front, lifelessly hitting the snow-covered ground the way a tossed sack would fall, having no order or control of itself. Phoebe pulled the horse's reins and screamed. Lee was startled and skittered his feet to a stop.

Phoebe and Cole got to Cyrus at the same time; he was face down in the snow. They turned him over and saw that his face was bluish and there was no breath. She pushed and pulled on his shirt, shaking him and yelling for him to get up. There was no response. Cole was frozen, staring. His friend was dead, there was no doubt.

...

Before placing the last stone on top of Cyrus's grave, Cole used it to pound a cross made of two sticks into the ground in front of it, then placed the stone gently on the pile. Phoebe's face was wet with tears, and she had not spoken in the hours since Cyrus had fallen over dead. Cole noticed for the first time how green her eyes were as they glistened with tears. She held onto her children and nodded to Cole, managing to squeak out, "Could you say something?"

Cole was not religious. He rarely paid any attention in mass, instead looking at Belinda if she were there, or thinking about her if she weren't. He knew no appropriate sermons or words that would be suitable for a moment like this. He stared at Phoebe blankly. She read his fear, but just nodded again at him in a fashion to say, 'Go ahead, it's OK.'

He folded his hands in the manner of prayer, trying to play his role, and decided to just talk about Cyrus. "Cyrus loved his family. He believed in his church and his mission. He was a man with a purpose and was not going to be bent from that purpose by anything, even if it killed him. I think that's pretty admirable and I'm lucky I got to know him."

Phoebe patted his shoulder in thanks and walked the kids away to the wagon. William looked back and asked, through tears, "So Daddy's stayin' here?"

"Yes, sweetie," Phoebe cried. "It's God's plan."

Cole stood and stared at the little cross. It looked so inadequate for the man that lay beneath it, who had so many hopes and dreams, a man with a passion for his wife and his purpose.

He thought about the scores of crosses they had passed and how this one would just blend in with the rest. He thought this one should be different but then realized that perhaps all those other crosses represented people with more depth than he had allowed himself to comprehend. Up until now, those crosses were warnings; cautions of the dangers all around him. Now, he realized each one marked the end of someone's hopes and dreams, and he was filled with a deep sadness.

...

They traveled just a few more miles that day, perhaps more to get away from the scene of Cyrus's death than for any purpose of progress. After the children went to sleep, Cole decided to speak with Phoebe about her plans. "Will you go on or turn back now?"

"I need to go on. There are people needing to be saved and it's God's plan that I do that now—and that William and Charity carry on that mission in the future." She looked seriously at Cole. "You know we aren't fools. We knew this could happen. We wouldn't have come all this way if I was just to turn back when ..." her voice broke as she thought of the words *Cyrus died*. Composing herself, she added, "You are part of God's plan now too. I need your help. I'm going to Salem in the Oregon Territory—the mission is there."

Cole had decided he was going to seek out a large river in the western part of Oregon, so that it was due north of California, where gold had been found. He did not know where Salem was but hoped it was on the way. He reached a hand out toward Phoebe and said, "Show me on the map where you are headed."

She spread the map out and held it facing the firelight, then pointed to the dot that represented Salem. It was in the west of the Oregon Territory and the dot was next to a long blue line. Cole pointed to the line and asked, "What's that?"

She looked closely at it. "It's the Willamette River. Salem sits on it."

Cole doubted that it was God's plan, but certainly felt this had happened for a reason. The Willamette would now be his destination.

…

A month passed and by their calculation on the map they were within two weeks of their destination. They had entered the sprawling Oregon Territory about three weeks ago. It had been a cold three weeks and today a blinding snowstorm halted their travels by early afternoon. It was evening now as Cole, Phoebe, William, and Charity huddled close together for warmth and rummaged for food to eat, using a few pieces of the remaining jerky they had stored since Missouri.

After eating they pulled the quilt back over them all for warmth. Just as they got warm, William said, "I have to pee," and they all laughed.

The storm raged through the night and cleared in the early hours. More than a foot of snow had been dumped. The plan for the day would be for Cole to ride Little Boy and Tusk would stay in the wagon. It was the only way to make forward progress.

By dusk, they judged that they had traveled perhaps fifteen miles when they came across a fast-moving stream that was not frozen and promised the potential for fish. So, they stopped to make camp. Cole set the net, cleared an area under some trees, and started a fire. No fish came by nightfall, and they went to bed hungry and cold. They tethered the horses in an area of dormant grass and cleared it as best they could so the horses could graze.

In the morning, there was a trapped river trout. They revived the fire, cooked up the trout, and ate hungrily. Tusk got the head and bones only but made no complaint. They trudged on silently after breakfast. Sticking up above the top of the snow in several places, they saw the tops of more stick crosses, marking travelers less fortunate than they were.

…

Over the course of the next week, they made increasing progress each day, in part due to lessening snow, as the storm seemed to hit less severely farther west, and in part due to their eagerness to reach Salem and replenish supplies. In seven days, they had caught three fish and snared one winter hare. The jerky was gone and the children, and Tusk, were whining for food. Cole and Phoebe had eaten sparingly during the week, allowing most of the food to go to the children.

They were roughly a week away from Salem and had not eaten all day when they settled in to sleep in the wagon. The fishnet and the snares were set, and they hoped for breakfast. William and Charity moaned with hungry bellies. Tusk whined, perhaps due to hunger, but he seemed more pained by the children's cries.

As daylight broke, Cole ran to the snares—nothing. Then to the net—he was devastated to see it empty. He had never known hunger in his life, but worse than his own hunger, he had to face the children and see their dejection.

He returned to the wagon and saw Phoebe looking hopefully at him. He gave a slight shake to his head and her shoulders slumped. They assumed their usual travel positions and got on their way. The children didn't even complain this time, which felt even worse to Cole and Phoebe. They were losing hope.

Cole thought about the crosses; how many were due to hunger? He and Phoebe had each eaten perhaps one full meal in seven days. They were weakening and moving slowly. He stumbled and fell to his knees several times during the morning. He was dizzy and the light was playing tricks on his eyes, sparkling around objects. His head had begun to hurt with a steady throb. Is this what it felt like to die? Is this how Cyrus felt weeks earlier?

Staggering forward, Cole's mind was racing through all of the events that led him here. "I've made such a mistake coming west," he said to himself, aloud. His own voice sounded like a stranger's to him, distant; echoing from a place beyond where he stood. Suddenly, he saw something coming at him from the corner of his eye and then felt a mighty blow to his entire left side. He was confused and could not identify what had struck him or where it came from. He could barely orient to where he was, but he suspected he was on the ground, facedown, as he felt slushy snow burning his cheek.

Phoebe was suddenly over him, but he didn't see where she came from. She sat him up and he began to come to his senses. Looking at Phoebe, he asked, "What hit me?"

She looked confused and then understood. "It was the ground. You just fell over and may not have even realized you were falling."

The ground. That's what he saw out of the corner of his eye. Fear gripped him and Cole sprang to his feet, as if to defy the grip of death on him and show that he had strength left to fight. He thought of Belinda and shuddered to think of her never knowing where he was—just another cross made of sticks somewhere in the Oregon Territory.

He turned to Phoebe and looked as strong as possible. "Let's keep moving. I'm OK now. But we need food today."

They moved on through the morning and into the early afternoon driven by a will to survive but with a growing fear they would not. Ahead, Cole saw a covered wagon stopped in the snow. It was pulled off to the right side of the trail but there were no marks in the snow, indicating it had been in this position since before the storm. Cole held a hand up to Phoebe, signifying that she should stop so he could investigate. He dismounted and called Tusk, who jumped eagerly from the back of the wagon. There was no sound from in the wagon and he could see the horse in front of the wagon, still tied in place, down on its knees in front and leaning to the left, propped up by the stave.

He called Tusk and waved him ahead, in case someone were to surprise him from inside the wagon. He called out but there was no reply, so he pulled a stick from the ground and used it to slide the back flap of the tented top open. Inside, he could make out two forms, lying side-by-side, a man and a woman. They were motionless. He called again and waited. Hearing nothing, and seeing no motion, he reached into the wagon with the stick and nudged one of them. Again, there was no response. Steeling his nerves, Cole climbed up on the back of the wagon and reached inside to check for breath. Both people were dead. It was a couple, perhaps in their late twenties or early thirties. Their eyes were still open, looking at each other. Cole guessed that one of them died and the other stared into their loved one's eyes, weak and dying themselves until they too passed. He thought to himself, *More hopes and dreams, dead.*

He waved Phoebe forward and called to her, "Two inside—a man and woman—dead. Starvation or exposure I suspect, though could have been illness. At any rate, they're gone." He looked in the back of the wagon, careful not to disturb the bodies too much, and found no food. Then he went to the front and to his surprise the horse was breathing but barely. He called back to Phoebe again. "The poor beast was stuck in the staves and could not free itself. It's dying—can't be saved. I'll have to put it out of its misery.

He took out his small knife and realized he would not be able to reach the large animal's heart quickly. The best way to end its suffering as quickly as possible would be to cut its throat. There would be a lot of blood, so he asked Phoebe to keep the kids in the wagon and look away. Cole knelt beside the horse and stroked its head. He whispered, "I'm sorry, boy," and jabbed his knife in the horse's neck and pulled it swiftly across, severing the throat at about three inches of depth and six inches across. The horse barely reacted. It just dropped its head within seconds and was dead.

Cole walked back to the Ryerson's wagon, his hands coated in blood. Phoebe poked her head out and looked at him pitifully. Then she looked past him and had an expression of hope. Cole spun around to follow her gaze, but nothing was there except the dead horse. It took him a moment to come to the same realization she had; the horse was the food that would carry them to Salem. It was more food than they could even hope to eat. He turned back to her, and she jumped from the wagon and embraced him.

Phoebe and William gathered wood for a large fire while Cole painstakingly carved portions of meat from the horse's body. As he worked, Cole thought about how different his life was now, how different he was now, to be able to rejoice in this meal with two dead people just a few feet away. *Hunger and fear of death change you quickly*, he thought.

They cooked enough meat to feed twenty adults. The children were contented and full. Tusk stopped eating while there was still more food to be had for the first time in his life. Phoebe and Cole smiled at each other and talked of their good fortune. Phoebe, of course, called it a gift from God. Cole didn't argue with her, but he could not understand how it could be a gift from God when two people and a horse died for it. Were the poor people in that wagon not in God's favor?

What they could not eat that night, they smoked overnight. Cole built a rack to lay the meat about three feet above the flames and fed the fire all night long, waking every hour or two to add fuel. By morning they had enough cooked meat to last their remaining trip three times over. They ate their fill again at breakfast then collected rocks for a crude burial of the two poor souls in the wagon. After hammering in two stick crosses, adding to the scores of them along the way to the Oregon Territory, they headed on their way, rejuvenated and ready for the final push.

…

They approached Salem, within the Oregon Territory from the north. The trail led south along the eastern bank of the Willamette River. Phoebe was at her destination as the mission she sought to join lay within Salem. Cole had some miles to go as he wanted to begin prospecting on the opposite bank and at least a full day's journey from Salem, so he would be less likely to run into local prospectors or outlaws.

As they arrived at the town, Cole stopped short and turned to Phoebe. "I'm not going into town. I want to head away and not lead others where I go."

Phoebe got down from the wagon and then lifted each of her children down. "We are going to say goodbye to Cole now, kids." Each child in turn gave Cole a hug, then moved on to Tusk to give him a longer, warmer hug, which amused the adults. As the smile trailed from Phoebe's face, she said, "I know that God put you in our path. My husband will always be the strongest and bravest man I ever met, but for us to find a worthy replacement to help guide us here, just as Cyrus was leaving this world, is too much for any coincidence. I'll remember you for the rest of my life."

The words touched Cole and he blushed, looked down, and replied, "I don't suppose either of us would have made it without the other. I'm so sorry for your loss and hope your mission work is all that you hoped."

He knew in that moment that Phoebe would remain one of the most important people in his memory for all his days, but that he may never see her again. She was strong and bold. He was certain he would have died on the journey without her. Cole remembered seeing her for the first time, a plain, nondescript woman in drab gray clothing and a bonnet. As he looked at her now, he saw beauty and strength. They embraced, saying no more, and then Cole turned quickly away to head south so that she would not see tears forming in his eyes.

March 1851 – Outside Salem, Oregon Territory

*I*t was an early March morning. Cole had traveled for more than five months and was finally at his destination, one of the many creeks and tributaries feeding the Willamette River in Western Oregon Territory. It made him smile that he had come all this way and was going to start working a creek that had no name. He had only known vaguely where he was headed when he set out from Cold Spring, New York, in the Hudson Valley. He reflected that it was like setting a leaf on fast-running water. You know the direction it will head but not the path it will take nor the place it will land. Where he stood now was in the direction he was headed, somewhere within an area of thousands of square miles he might have gone to within the Oregon Territory, but this looked as good a spot as any for gold to hide and in truth, no one knew where it was anyway, or they'd have gotten it already. He was truly on his own now. There was no town, and perhaps no people, within twenty miles. He could get to Salem in a day when he needed provisions or if he were injured but able to travel. He hoped to only make that trek to bring his bounty to the refinery and get paid.

He pulled the gold pan that Joseph Mills had given him from where it was tied onto Little Boy and walked down to the waterside at the creek. He felt like it was his first day of school and he wouldn't know the answers to the teacher's questions. He was grateful to be completely alone now and have no one see his feeble attempts at finding gold.

Still, he had a core optimism about him, and he said aloud to himself, "Let's find some gold and get back home." The temperature was surprisingly comfortable for February. Joseph had told him that the Pacific Northwest was warmer than back home in New York. This had the feel of a crisp late March morning back home. The sky was overcast but he had decent light to work with. The creek was good-sized, and the water flowed steadily. It was no more than a foot deep in most places and perhaps fifteen feet across. It looked like what he imagined when he thought about panning for gold. The ground sloped gently up on each side, clear for the first fifty feet or so, and then wooded beyond that. Even in the muted light of the overcast sky, the water glistened as it bent back and forth through the rocky terrain, like a silver ribbon.

Cole took his first dip into the creek bed with Joseph's gold pan, pulling up water, pebbles, and sand. He felt like there should be more ceremony to this moment, after all this time. He swirled the mixture counterclockwise and let the water and larger pieces spill over the edge as he'd been shown. There was no glitter, so he dipped and did it again. He repeated the process for four hours before taking a break for a midday meal. While he had been panning, he had seen several fish swim by, so he decided to set his net for the afternoon. A trout would be ideal for dinner to break the steady diet of horse meat.

He and Phoebe had split the remaining smoked meat from the horse, so he had a supply that would still last him days. He had panned from just below his camp, upstream about two hundred yards. After lunch, he would try to cover the same ground heading downstream for his position. Within a couple of days, he would have to move camp, to avoid the extra hike to where he would be panning. His plan was to move about a mile upstream every couple of days. He would pan both sides of the stream looking for flakes of gold, coming from strains up one of the slopes from the creek, driven over time by gravity, erosion, and rainwater down into the creek bed.

That afternoon he started panning again, dip after dip, swirl after swirl. He wondered what it would be like to actually see gold flecks and he convinced himself that the next one would show the elusive metal. It didn't. The day ended and he was tired. His back ached from hunching over the water and repeatedly picking up sand, rocks, and water. Tusk had been lying by the side of the creek, occasionally lapping the fresh, bubbling water and chasing a squirrel when the chance arose. "You're no help at all, are you, boy?" Cole said with a smile, and Tusk cocked his head as he always did at questions.

Cole knew the odds of finding gold on his first day were low. From all he had been told, finding it at any point was going to be a challenge. All the same, he felt a pang of discouragement. Something in this journey felt like destiny at this point. If his goals were pure, saving Belinda's farm, and in doing so saving her family, then surely, he had to have some advantage over the hundreds of other men rushing to the hills for fortunes that they wanted for lust or greed. Then he thought, the reasons may not matter in the end, but work and perseverance will. Resolving himself to work until the job was done, he made his camp ready for supper and sleep.

In two days, Cole had panned a half mile each, up and downstream from his camp. He pulled up stakes and headed upstream a mile. He had no luck with snares but had netted fish just about as often as he liked. On his second day, he set the net, and a fish was in it before he even walked away. He took it out and filleted it there and reset the net, catching another within the hour. He was feeling optimistic about the food supply, though it was likely going to be fish for every meal once the smoked horse meat was gone.

. . .

After a week of working his way upstream, the moderate-sized stream had now become a narrow trickle. He had run out of room on this feeder stream. He had not caught a fish in the past two days, in the dwindling waterway, so he used up the rest of his smoked meat. He shared the final bits of horse meat with Tusk and packed up to seek the next stream that fed the large Willamette River.

He had hiked about two hours up the west side of Willamette River when he came to a good-sized tributary. The mouth of the stream was a good thirty feet across, which was promising, as he would likely be able to follow this for many miles away from the river before it became too small to be worth panning. He decided to begin at the mouth and pan all day before choosing a camp location. He also decided that rather than traversing the waterway to pan both sides as he went along, he would only work the southern edge as he worked his way upstream and then work the northern side when he turned at the narrow end of the stream in several days. This would save time, not wading across, and he would cover a little more than twice the straight-line distance each day and then similar on his return. It would also save him the hike back to the river. He calculated that he would have saved a half day with this tactic on the prior creek.

Today was the first day that the full sun had broken through the overcast sky. Cole was learning that the Oregon Territory was a gloomy place, absent of sun most of the time and a light rain falling at some point almost daily. In the brighter light of sun, he had several moments of false hope. A white stone would glint, or some other mineral would sparkle in the light and his heart would leap, only to be disappointed a moment later.

Tusk let out a bark and stared across the Willamette River. They were still close enough to the mouth of the tributary creek to see the river fully. Cole followed the dog's gaze and saw motion in the bushes across the water on the east bank. Two men emerged and did not at first see Cole, but another bark from Tusk alerted them. It was difficult to make out their faces, but both men wore full beards, and one was taller than the other by almost a head and broader as well. They each waved a hand overhead in an exaggerated fashion, due to the distance of two hundred feet or so that separated them. "Hello there," The shorter man bellowed.

Cole waved.

"Any luck?" the man yelled.

"Nothing yet." Cole thought to himself that his answer would have been the same even if he'd already found gold.

"You out here alone?"

Cole hesitated. "Nah. My partner's up the creek a ways." Better to be safe with folks he didn't know.

The shorter man continued. "We're headed to Salem. Been at it for a month and need a real bed and someone to share it." The larger man let out a laugh, then the smaller one closed with, "Good luck."

Cole waved and watched them leave. He didn't feel any risk from them as the river would be difficult to cross here and he likely didn't look like he had anything worth stealing, if they were outlaws looking for money or gold. He bent down and scooped up water and creek-bottom sand in his pan.

The days were long and monotonous. Cole kept his mind occupied by imagining his triumphant return to Cold Spring. In his daydream he would be riding Little Boy toward the farm, Belinda would be coming in from the fields and see him. She would drop the tools in her hand and run to him. She was wearing a sundress and sweat caused it to grip her body tightly. After a long, passionate kiss and embrace, he would open his rucksack and show her a pile of money for the farm and a single gold nugget that he had saved for her.

Back in his reality of prospecting, his movements had become mechanical, and halfway through the day he had little recollection of the distance he had covered. He wondered if even finding gold would have broken his trance. There was a fat river trout in his net, which was a small victory in the absence of gold. He built a small fire to cook the fish and eat. Tusk came running, eager to do his part.

March 1851 – Cold Spring, New York

Cole had been gone more than half a year and Belinda felt so changed that she hoped he would see her the same way and hold the same passion for her when he returned. Six months felt more like six years to her. She had become the head of her household and learned to manage the farm; assigning chores, planting, harvesting, and negotiating prices for crops. She was proud of what she had accomplished but she felt old and tired, and she missed Cole. He had loved Belinda the girl, would he love Belinda the woman? She wondered. She would also lay awake wondering how he may have changed when, if, he returned. Will he still have the bright look in his eyes that she loved so much?

They had made enough with the fall harvest to survive the winter. With the banknote paid last fall and due again this fall, she had set her goal to be as self-sufficient as possible on the farm, so that this year's fall harvest would pay the next installment. If they shifted to corn as the only crop, as she and Cole had planned, due to the extra labor needed on wheat, they would be perilously close to disaster. They might have to choose between paying the banknote and having enough money for food the next winter. She could not count on Cole returning with gold or money. She had to act.

It was a Saturday in mid-March and Belinda called a family meeting after the morning chores and breakfast were complete. Her mother, Alice, and Buck all sat, eyes on her, awaiting whatever decision or direction she would offer. She reflected on how strange it was that they had all accepted this new reality. It had never been spoken of or overtly granted that she was in charge, it just came to be, naturally.

Looking alternately at Alice and Buck with a level expression and calm voice, she began. "We made it through winter with what money we had left, after paying the bank, and the food we stored. You've been a great help, and everyone has pulled their weight."

The room felt heavy with anticipation. Buck looked nervously over at Alice, who shot a glance back. Mama sat still. No one spoke.

"Last fall Alice stayed out of school until we got through the harvest and setting the farm to order. Buck went from the start and you've both been in school since Alice went back. Miss Roundtree says you both do good work. Mama and I are so proud." Belinda nodded to her mother, who agreed and put a hand on each child's knee to show her appreciation. Then, Belinda paused and took a deep breath, continuing, "I need to take you both out of school for the rest of this year. We never plowed the wheat under, and it has been coming up nicely. We had planned to convert to corn but we need the higher price we get for wheat in order to survive. We can't afford a farm hand so it's just us and we can't get the corn fields ready for planting, plus bring in the wheat harvest without all four of us working. On top of that, the vegetable garden will have to be made larger and planted this month so we can feed ourselves without using as much money from the crops."

Alice groaned and looked downcast, while Buck smiled and said, "Is that all? I don't care about school. I thought somebody'd died or somethin'."

"I've talked to Miss Roundtree and gotten some books and your assignments from school. I'll be working with you five nights each week for two hours. We aren't going to let you fall behind."

Alice nodded understanding but her eyes were glassy; she would miss her friends at school. Buck slumped in his chair, disappointed that his hopes of an early summer vacation were dashed. It was agreed and they ended the meeting with a group hug, something Belinda had instituted to confirm their agreements.

April 1851 – Salem, Oregon Territory

The days ran together. Even the weather rarely changed here—gray overcast with misty rain off and on. But Cole was thankful that it was moderate, with winter behind him. The routine repeated daily; he awoke at the first crack of light, ate a bit of fish cooked the night before, ambled down to the water, checked his fishnet and snares, panned for gold all day, moved upstream, and set camp for another day. He kept track of the days by notching a stick to keep count. He had entered April, he was sure, but he could not be sure of the exact day. Over the course of more than seven months now, since leaving home, he had missed marking days and just tried to keep close to the week or month he was in.

The work itself was maddening; bend, scoop, swirl, stare, dump, repeat. Cole had figured that he did it about three to four times each minute for close to ten hours each day. More than two thousand times each day for a month. He figured out the number of months it would take to reach one million scoops—a little less than a year and a half—and then shuddered at the thought of being gone that long. How long could he keep at this without a hint of gold?

It was a cool morning. Cole awoke with a start and immediately felt that he'd been dreaming, and something in that dream had woken him, but he rarely remembered dreams and could not call himself back to this one. He looked out across his small campsite and down toward the water. He was back to the Willamette River, and it was time to find another tributary to pan. This would be his fourth creek and he began to feel hopeless. He told himself that one month wasn't a long time to be prospecting, and he knew that to be true, but he could not shake a low feeling.

He looked into his sack at what money he had remaining. Three dollars, two quarters, and four pennies. It was a preciously small sum, and he knew that finding gold was not now just about saving the farm. He needed more funds for a trip home.

Cole looked over at Tusk and began to speak with him. It was something he did more and more often during the trip. He found that the sound of talking helped with being alone. He also was amused by how Tusk would cock his head to one side as if straining to hear so he could understand. "OK, boy, here's the situation. We've got about three and a half dollars and probably shouldn't go stay in Salem for a night. We need to save that. But I'm gonna go crazy if I don't, and we've got to check out the gold refinery we heard about there, to see if we think we can trust them when we find a big pile of gold." He paused as if waiting for the dog to answer. "OK then, it's settled. We go to Salem today." Cole smiled and tussled Tusk's head.

The morning seemed to brighten for Cole. He needed a change after a month of bending, scooping, swirling thousands of times each day. He hiked north along the west bank of the Willamette, taking note along the way of other tributaries he would circle back to and pan. Ahead, he caught sight of a black bear moving slowly along the water. Tusk saw too and Cole was too late to grab him. The dog was off in a shot, barking. Cole stood frozen, imagining a gruesome end for his companion, but to his surprise and amusement, the bear turned and ran, full speed toward the woods on the left. He easily outpaced the little dog and Tusk gave up the chase and returned, looking triumphant.

Late in the morning, they reached their destination. Through the course of moving north to new tributaries, they had gotten to within twelve miles of Salem, so the trip was shorter than Cole had expected. Seeing the town ahead on his right, Cole remembered he was on the wrong side of the water. A short distance ahead he saw a young boy, perhaps fourteen, sitting by the shore. He had a raft tied up and when he saw Cole approaching, he stood up quickly and picked up a long stick Cole assumed was for poling across. He was wearing overalls and a gray shirt that had been patched at the elbows. He was slim and had dirty blond hair to his shoulders. "I'll take you and the dog across for twenty-five cents," the boy shouted as they approached. "The horse'll have to swim. It ain't deep by the edges and he could walk a good part of the way."

Cole had crossed at a fairly low spot in the river when he left Phoebe and headed past the town a month ago. He thought about doing so again but he didn't have time to allow his clothes to dry and he wanted to get a meal and a room, so he dug out a quarter, looked at it for a moment, realizing how his money supply was dwindling, then handed it over. He hopped on board, but Tusk looked wary as the eight-by-eight-foot raft floating a few feet from the riverbank. Not willing to be left behind, he hopped on and squatted low, balancing himself. Cole shook his head, saying, "You'll chase a bear, but this is what scares you." He held Little Boy's lead and the horse walked next to the raft as the young ferryman poled them across. As the ground gave way, the horse swam instinctively.

Arriving in town, Cole saw the now-familiar sights, from his travels west, of a town consisting of a main thoroughfare, lined with buildings of various shapes and sizes. Horses, carts, and men milled about, doing business, getting food and drink, and speaking with women with heavily painted faces like Priscilla from Pittsburgh. He asked a passing stranger, "Where is the gold refinery?"

The man was tall and gaunt looking, in his thirties, with a pronounced Adam's apple, dark hair, and a stubbly face with sharp features. His face lit up. "You found gold!" It was a statement, not a question, and he turned excitedly as if to yell the news to others.

Cole grabbed his arm. "No—no. I just want to talk to them for when I do."

The man tipped his head back and looked appraisingly at Cole, down his sharp nose. "You just don't want nobody to know where the gold is—keep it for yourself, I understand."

Fearing he had made a mistake; Cole pulled his rucksack off of Little Boy and opened it. "Sir, I have no gold. I've found not a single fleck in a month of panning. I wish what you're saying were true, but I've found nothing." He paused, "But I'll never give up and I want to know what to do when I do find it, that's all."

The man looked circumspect still and spoke slowly now, as if thinking about each word. "Well, I was just hopeful. Ain't nobody findin' shit. They set up that refinery hopin' to get the gold when it comes, but they'll have plenty of time to talk for now, cuz there ain't been none. It's on the other end of town, yonder." He pointed down the main road.

Cole walked through town and passed an inn that looked decent. He decided to get situated so he could put Little Boy and Tusk in a stable and complete his business. He lashed Little Boy to a post and stepped into the inn. It looked like the others he had stayed in, though no music played at this late morning hour. To his right in the tavern, there was a single patron, looking asleep with his head on the bar, and a smattering of empty tables. To his left, a desk for checking into rooms that were up a narrow stairway with a low railing. At the desk was a small man in his forties wearing a loose-fitting white shirt and brown trousers too big around the waist but cinched up with a belt that pinched the material around him and made the pants look like a sack that was loosely filled and tied closed at the top. Sandy-brown, wavy hair hung past his ears, and he wore small, round, wire-framed glasses.

He sprung to his feet, appearing excited for the business. "Good day, I am John, how can I help you, good sir?" He sounded overly formal and spoke crisply.

Cole smiled and nodded. "I'd like a room and would like to stable my horse."

"Splendid. That will be a dollar and fifty cents," the man said cheerfully, smiling eagerly back at Cole.

This was more costly than Cole's other stops. It would leave him less than two dollars. He glanced around the empty bar, wondering if he should sleep outside and save the money, but he desperately needed a break in his routine.

Sensing a customer slipping away, John asked, "Where have you traveled from?"

"New York state, about seven months back. I've been here a month."

"That's quite a journey, but you made good time for traveling in winter. Most folks travel in the warmer months and still take six months or more comin' from that far east." He paused and looked up at his rooms, mostly empty. "How about one dollar for the room, with breakfast? You can stable the horse and dog yourself, as I don't have a stable boy at the moment, and it would save me doing it. When the gold comes, we'll have more steady business, but the bar is lively at night so be sure to be here."

Cole pulled a dollar out and paid, thanking John, though he didn't want to let on how badly in need of this he felt. He was ashamed that the idea of a bed for the night and conversations with people in the bar later that evening had such a hold on him. It felt like weakness to him.

After removing the saddle and supplies from Little Boy, Cole left him with some water and fresh hay at the stable, then headed to the refinery, carrying his rucksack, with Tusk following. The refinery was set near the water, but at the north end of town, while he had entered from the south end. Across the dirt roadway from the inn, Cole saw the man with the prominent Adam's apple leaning against the front of the railing by the general store. He was not looking in Cole's direction, but something felt odd, as if he were looking away intentionally, trying to seem casual.

Cole walked on and glanced back a few times, but the man didn't leave his spot. On his left, he saw a familiar sight from every town he'd passed through, the brothel. Young girls, and a few older ladies, painted in the fashion that apparently appealed to other men, waved and bared their breasts to get the attention of would-be customers.

Near the end of town, on the right, was the mission headquarters where Phoebe was destined when he had left her. Cole was eager to check in on her and see William and Charity as well. He stepped inside and saw an older man at a desk. He was dressed in a similar drab gray cloth that Cyrus had worn. He wore glasses and had a circle of gray hair around the sides of his head with a shiny bald head on top.

"I'd like to see Phoebe Ryerson, please," Cole said, noticing he had instinctively folded his hands together as if he were in church.

The man rose to his feet but was barely taller than when seated, as he hunched over sharply in the center of his back. Looking over the top of his glasses, he replied, "I'm afraid you'll seldom find her here. She is a whirlwind, that one. She is always out with the native folk, and she's brought more to the faith than any five men we've had here before."

Cole smiled, unsurprised at the response, thanked the man, then headed to the refinery.

The refinery was a set of two buildings. In the rear, the actual refinery where gold would be melted and formed into bars or coins for transit, and the front building that looked much like any other storefront in town, except for two large, rough-looking men with shotguns out front. The refinery building had no windows or doors and could only be accessed by first passing through the store out front.

Cole nodded to the two guards, who barely acknowledged him, then walked inside. Tusk had become accustomed to waiting outside for Cole. He sat down in front of one of the guards and stared up at him, which made Cole smile as he walked in. *Doesn't fear bears, nor big men with guns,* he thought to himself.

The man behind the counter was in his fifties, with gray hair and a clean-shaven, round face. He wore a leather visor and spectacles hung around his neck. He looked up when Cole entered and immediately glanced down at his rucksack, obviously expecting, or at least hoping, that it contained gold. He spoke in a hoarse voice, "The name's Tom. Ya got some gold to measure there?"

Cole shook his head and saw the disappointment on the man's face. "I'm Cole, I have been at it a month, but I'll be back with gold, I promise you that. I want to know how it will work when I do find it and bring it here."

"They all say they'll find gold, but few do. I wish you luck though." The man said, slowly shaking his head. He slid off of his stool and pulled a scale from under the counter to demonstrate. "If you bring me gold, I'll weigh the rocks here. Mind you, it won't be pure gold, so I'll have to separate the gold from the rock you find it in. Some folks think they have half a pound and it's only two or three ounces. They get mad like I made the rocks." He lifted his hands and shrugged.

Cole smiled. He liked Tom instantly and his instincts told him this would be a trustworthy man to do business with. There were gold buyers outside of refineries too. They promised on-the-spot payment but paid less than a refinery would.

"If you bring your gold to me, I'll get you a fair price. I pay next day, cuz I have to test it and weigh it all. It'll take a couple of days longer if you hit really big, as I don't keep more cash on-site than I need to, and it comes by armed coach twice each week."

Cole nodded, shook his hand, looked Tom in the eye, and said, "I'll be back with gold. I don't know when, but I will."

Tom smiled, and through a slight chuckle, replied, "Ya know, kid, something makes me believe that. Good luck to you. Watch out for outlaws. They always watch for who might have made a find and they'll poach it. They'll kill you for an ounce."

Cole returned to the inn and brought Tusk to stay in the stable. He planned to leave him with Little Boy so he could go to his room to rest before supper. The pen door was open slightly, but he was relieved to see that Little Boy had not walked out. He was sure he had closed it. Inside the stall, he looked with horror at the emptiness. All of his supplies were gone—the saddle, the repaired burlap tent cover, his lone frying pan and his prospecting tools, including the gold pan and the small pickaxe that he would need when he located gold and needed to dislodge it from the ground. He looked about wildly to see if anyone was nearby. He immediately thought of the stranger he had asked about the refinery, who he was sure had been watching him leave the inn earlier. Flinging open his rucksack, he saw the dismal remainder of his supplies, a change of clothes, his fishnet, twine, a flint, and the needle he had used to repair the burlap cover.

The loss was devastating. He could not survive, living at least a month at a time in the wild, without his frying pan to cook fish and his cover to protect him from the elements as he slept. If he did survive, he couldn't seek gold without his tools. Cole thundered into the inn and approached John who immediately stepped back, sensing his rage. "All of my things were stolen from your stable." He looked expectantly at the small man, who showed genuine surprise.

"Son, I am sorry but there's a bad element out here." He held his hands up in front of himself in the universal sign of surrender.

"You have to replace everything I lost," Cole said incredulously.

"Well, hold on there." John kept his hands up. "I told you I had no stable boy and didn't charge you for storing your horse there. I can't watch everything." Seeing the devastation in Cole's eyes, he added, "I truly am sorry for you."

Rest was no longer on the agenda. He had to look for his things or look to replace them. He went outside and looked up and down the road. The reality set in immediately that who-ever took his supplies, probably the man with the prominent Adam's apple, wouldn't be here now. He walked the length of the town, even moving down alleys and behind buildings, but found nothing besides a man fucking one of the women from the brothel and another getting sucked off. He even saw a man sucking another man behind the saloon, but no sign of the stranger or his things.

Dejected, he went to the general store. Replacing his flint, tent cover, frying pan, and gold dish were his priorities. He would live with no saddle as he walked Little Boy most of the time, using him to carry supplies more than himself. He would wait on a pickaxe until he found gold. He gathered the supplies in silence, staring vacantly as he filled his arms, then brought them to the counter. The shopkeeper tapped each item and moved his lips silently counting. "That'll be two dollars and seventy-five cents". It was more than Cole had left. He turned and left the store empty handed without any response to the man at the counter.

Sitting on the porch of the inn, Cole had no memory of the walk back from the general store. He had left the needed supplies there to think. His mind raced but no solutions came. Time moved and he realized it was getting dark. He had not eaten all day and the inn was now bustling inside. People must have been walking by him to go into the bar for the past hour or two, but he had seen no one in his fog of despair. Tusk was curled up by him. Cole walked him back to the stable, empty, but for his horse, and closed the animals in together.

Entering the bar, Cole heard the familiar sounds of every tavern—piano keys now tinkled out an upbeat melody and the notes hung in the air with the smell of beer and sweat. Women with heavily painted faces and breasts forced up by bras, so that looked like they were trying to escape out of low-cut dresses, circled the floor in search of paying customers. The bar seats were full and three of the tables had card games already going. The occasional hoot of joy, followed by a "Goddammit," rang out across the room.

A woman in a low-cut red dress with black lace around a plunging neckline that revealed most of her breasts walked toward Cole. He looked up and simply said, "I have no money." His look of desperation likely convinced her more than even the words he spoke; she walked past. The table farthest from the bar and nearest to the piano had three men seated, playing cards. Something made Cole look closer at them.

Seated on the left side was a slim man in his thirties with a well-worn leather hat. He had light brown hair just past his ears and a thin, scraggly beard that covered his face like wispy fuzz, still leaving the skin below perfectly visible. He wore a dirty blue shirt under overalls. In the center, facing Cole, was a stocky, strong-looking man in his twenties with a thick, long black beard. He wore a flannel shirt and had the rugged look of a man used to the outdoors. Cole mused as to whether he himself had such a look now. The man wore a thin leather rope around his neck with a large tooth hanging from it, probably from a bear. To the right was a large man, perhaps in his late twenties but looked older. Even seated, it was clear he would tower over the other two. He also had a thick dark beard, though not completely black. He was laughing at what the middle-seated man said and his grin showed a missing upper tooth left of center. He wore a flannel shirt that looked like it took the material of two normal-sized shirts to make. A large hunting knife sat on the table by his right hand.

As Cole studied the men, the man in the center called to him. "Hey, friend, you made it to town."

Cole paused and obviously looked confused because the man added, "We saw you across the river a while back. Had any luck yet?"

"Oh … I remember now … no. Well, I guess you could say I've had luck, but it's all been bad."

"That's the kind of luck we have 'round here," the man said, which drew a hearty laugh from the big man. "Where's your partner at?"

Again, Cole registered confusion, before remembering his lie. "Oh, he stayed at camp." Adding after another awkward pause, "So we'll always have someone working."

The man stared at him, studying him, then said, "OK, friend." He was no longer smiling. After a pause, he smiled again and said, "Join the game, we need a fourth."

"I'm almost out of money. I haven't even eaten, so I'm sorry, I can't."

"It's penny ante, and like my daddy used to say, 'The man with nothin' left's got nothin' left to lose.'" The big man roared with laughter again.

"Nothing left to lose," echoed Cole, softly, to himself. A flood of thoughts poured into his mind. He thought of Emit Wright—had he felt he had nothing left to lose? Did every gambler think they had to do it? But what if he did win a little—and go buy his supplies? Could this be what keeps his dream alive and allowed him to save the farm and his life there with Belinda? What would his mother think if he gambled away the last of his money? Then his mind returned to the phrase— "The man with nothing left has nothing left to lose."

Cole looked at the three faces staring at him, unsure of how long he had paused, shook his head as if clearing the fog, then replied, "OK, I'll play a little."

The man in the center said, "Damn, friend. I thought your mind left and forgot to take your body with it for a moment there." The big man laughed heartily again at his friend's wit.

The black-bearded man, who was apparently the spokesman of the group, made the introductions. He pointed to the man in the leather hat. "This here's Jacques. He's Canadian—a fur trapper, like us, dabbling in some gold prospecting as well. We just met Jacques today and convinced him to join us for a game. He don't say much." Waving a hand toward the big man, he continued, "This moving mountain here is Burl. He's my partner in trappin'. It's good havin' a big fella around in the wild. I'd guess even a bear might think twice before goin' at him. I'm Levi but folks call me Lev. My parents picked a name they didn't think could be shortened, but I just took that as a challenge." Burl let out another full-throated laugh at that, even though he'd likely heard that explanation many times.

The three men dropped pennies on the table. Cole reached into his rucksack for his money. He could see that Lev was paying close attention as he removed four pennies and a quarter. He placed them in a stack in front of himself, then slid his penny into the center of the table. He had never gambled for anything other than sunflower seeds. He felt the weight of the moment, as if he were venturing into a land where he had never traveled. Then the cards came, and he just played.

Burl's face was an almost comical canvas of every emotion he felt. He picked his cards up one at a time, registering happiness or disappointment with each, as he lightly bit his tongue that stuck out of the left side of his mouth. Jacques and Lev gave no such obvious clues as to their fortunes.

Cole looked down at his first hand, a smattering of numbers and suits. Jack high would be a certain loser, so after Burl passed without betting, Cole did as well. Jacques raised a penny then Lev and Burl both added their pennies to stay in. Cole folded, unwilling to concede more money on the random chance of the draw. Now he watched. He needed to learn how each man played. He knew how Dale played, and he had seen how people played along the road as he watched, but now he had money at stake—his future was at stake.

Burl traded three cards in: Jacques two and Lev one. Based on Burl's general demeanor and inability to hide any emotion on his face, Cole assumed he had stayed in just on hope and that hope would likely not lead to any more than the thousands of swirls of Cole's gold pan. As Burl looked at his three new cards, the suspicion was confirmed. Jacques likely had a pair and high card that he held onto, hoping to match it with one of his draws. It was unlikely he had drawn three of a kind to start, but possible. Lev may have had four cards toward a straight or flush, but more likely two pair.

Burl opened the next round of betting and tossed in two

pennies. He flashed the other players a confident look that Cole would have found funny if it were not so sad in its transparency. This man was giving away money and the others had to know that too. Jacques studied Lev, not even looking at Burl, then put in his two pennies. Cole thought to himself, *if he knows what he is doing, that would mean he landed a second pair on his draw.* Lev called the two cents, not raising more, likely thinking the same thing Cole did.

Burl turned over his hand full of nothing—king high. Jacques produced a pair of tens and an ace high. So, Cole thought, he hadn't pulled a second pair and he either missed that Lev likely did have two pair or perhaps he thought it was a bluff. Lev flipped his hand—a pair of twos, a pair of sevens, and a jack.

Cole felt a rush of satisfaction. For a single penny, he had learned that he had one completely inept player at the table, one who understood the game but may not read situations fully, and one who was smart but careful. He hoped the investment would pay off during the evening.

After about a dozen hands, Cole had yet to play one to the end. He had made it to the draw a few times but in all of those hands, he saw imminent defeat and cut his losses. He was down almost a quarter; money he could not afford to lose. It dawned on him that cards were a little like prospecting for gold. You have to keep bending and dipping and eventually, you find your treasure. Unfortunately, like his prospecting, he had not found it yet.

On the next hand, he found a potential gold flake, Two jacks, an ace, eight, and three. All of the cards were black. Four spades, with the second jack being a club. He had three ways to play the hand. First, he could dump the jack of clubs and take a chance at a flush. Second, he could trade three cards looking for a third jack. Third, he could trade two cards, keeping the ace high, hoping to pair it with a draw. He ruled out the third option immediately as it was unlikely there would be another pair of jacks, where the ace high would break the tie and he would rather give himself three shots at the third jack. He then decided against putting all of his hopes on one card coming back as a spade. He figured that there were forty-seven cards he had not seen and only nine spades were left. Worse than a one-in-five chance. He was the third to play this hand with Lev and Burl deciding before him, but first would be the betting.

Lev led with two pennies and Burl matched it, as he always did. Cole matched, not wanting to invest too heavily until the draw, nor did he want to give away any confidence he had in the hand. Jacques raised it to four cents. Lev studied Jacques's face and then put his two more cents in to match. Burl followed suit and Cole wondered if Burl was able to do anything without following Lev's lead. Cole thought about the odds. Right now, with a pair of the fourth highest cards, he was not better than fifty-fifty to win this hand. But the pot would be twenty cents with him in and he had a chance. He added two more pennies.

Lev and Burl both traded three cards and Cole did the same. Jacques traded one. Cole watched each man intently as they took their cards. Burl's disappointment was so obvious that Cole was able to focus on the other two quickly. There was a faint flash of disappointment on Jacques's face, and he felt sure he was playing off of two pair or taking a swing at a straight or flush. Lev gave away nothing. Cole picked up his cards and saw what he was looking for, a jack, between a ten and six. He had three jacks. He was confident he had Jacques and Burl beaten, but Lev was an unknown.

Lev opened the betting by passing and Burl looked mournfully at his cards and passed as well. Cole had to move here. There was a risk if he passed that Jacques would do so as well, and they would all just flip cards with the pot staying as it was. He needed to win more while he had a good hand. He bet ten cents.

Jacques looked startled and looked back at his hand. He had lost earlier to two pair, and now Cole felt sure that's what he was looking down at in his own hands. It would be hard for him to lay down that hand, even if he should. Cole hoped it would lead him to bet his hand. Jacques tossed ten cents into the pot. Lev was staring into Cole's eyes. He never even glanced at the other two men at the table. It was clear he had read the situation as Cole had. Cole thought to himself, *If he has a pair, he will lay it down now for sure. If he bets this, he has three of a kind like I do and it's just a matter of whose is higher.*

Lev reached into his pocket and pulled out two one-dollar liberty coins. Staring into Cole's eyes, he tossed them in the center of the table where they clanged on the other coins like a railroad hammer hitting a spike. Burl threw his cards down, declaring, "I'm out," then added, "Best if y'all did the same. I seen that look in Lev's eye before and he's got ya." Lev threw a sharp look at Burl, who cast his eyes down and quieted himself.

Cole said, "I thought this was penny ante," stalling for time.

Lev looked back at him with a level gaze. "That's the ante, sure, but we ain't set no limit on bets, did we, boys?"

Burl took the opportunity to recover from the scolding look, agreeing readily with an exaggerated shake of his head and a quick, "No, sir, we did not."

Cole could see that Jacques had already thrown his cards down, not willing to wager two more dollars on his two-pair hand even though his turn had not come. Lev likely had three of a kind and they likely were high enough to encourage him that they would beat Cole's if he also had three. So, were they nines or tens, or one of the three cards higher than jacks? It was as if Cole's entire life had come down to this hand; come down to luck, or perhaps fate. His supplies had been stolen. He could no longer prospect for gold without supplies, or money to replace them. If he won this hand, he could afford to carry on. His dreams wouldn't die, yet. He could also fold here and play on, but his odds were not likely going to be better on any hand than he had now. There was always a risk of loss.

Cole looked back across the table, meeting Lev's gaze, and said, "The man with nothing left ... well, you know how the rest goes." Cole reached into his rucksack and let his fingers close around his last two one-dollar coins, feeling their weight as he withdrew them. Every sense was heightened in this moment as he felt the cool edges of the metal on his skin, heard the soft clank of the coins against each other, and finally saw the gleam of the silver as he opened his hand to place them in the center of the table. "Call."

Jacques folded immediately and Lev showed a touch of fear

as he turned his cards. He stared directly into Cole's eyes looking to read his reaction. Three tens, an ace, and a seven. Burl let out a whoop and slapped his hand excitedly on the table.

Things happen for a reason, Cole thought. *This game was here to save me, and it has.* His shoulders relaxed, letting go of a tension he had not even been aware of, then he laid the cards on the table. Seeing he had lost, Lev let out a loud "Goddammit." His face reddened and his fists clenched. It was a common outburst in all the games Cole had watched but this felt different. Lev looked like a man unaccustomed to losing. He looked like a dam ready to burst. His eyes at that moment looked familiar to Cole but he couldn't place why.

Cole reached out his hands to pull back his winnings, but Burl grabbed his large hunting knife and in a quick motion, brought it down on the wood table just beyond Cole's right hand. The eight-inch blade plunged a full inch deep into the soft wood. Cole stared at the knife, too afraid to move. It was a Jim Bowie knife, finely crafted with a carved wood handle. The world seemed to pause, and the room went quiet.

After a long pause, a shaky voice came through the silence. "Is everything alright over here, gentlemen?" It was John, the small innkeeper.

Lev unclenched his fists, opening a broad smile on his face, that lacked any sincerity. "We're just havin' a friendly game over here. The young buck here won a big hand and we're congratulatin' him, that's all."

Taking the opportunity with the innkeeper present, Cole added, "Ya, we were just finishing up. I'm going to get some food and turn in." He pulled the money towards him, gathered it and stuffed it in his sack, then rose to his feet.

"Oh, we don't want the fun to end." Lev smiled. "Plus, it's only right to let me have a shot at winning some of my money back."

Cole nodded toward the knife, firmly planted in the table, "I think that was all the fun I can handle for one night." Then he turned and walked away.

The smile left Lev's face as he called out, "Hope to meet your partner someday."

...

Cole got little sleep that night. He kept seeing the deadly look in Lev's eyes. He expected Lev and Burl to come through the door and attack him at any moment, but that moment never came. At daybreak, he checked on the animals and headed to the general store. He purchased only what he needed for that moment, leaving the saddle and pickaxe for another time when he needed to wrench gold from the ground and then ride back east. He wrapped his supplies in the burlap tent cover he had just purchased, using some twine to cinch it shut, then slung it over Little Boy's back. It took a few minutes to get the weight right, as it hung down both sides, so it would not fall off easily, but he did not intend to go fast, and it worked well enough.

As he left town, he decided to stay on the eastern side of the river to prospect this time—it would make it easier to get to town the next time he came, hopefully with gold. He also decided to head north. Lev and Burl had seen his last location, and he wanted a better chance that they would not stumble upon him. He traveled a full day, putting more than twenty miles of wilderness between himself and Salem and, more importantly, between himself and two men he felt confident would do him harm if given a chance. Reflecting on the night before, he realized why Lev's look had felt familiar to him. He looked like Tommy when he glared at Cole across the grave site, with a murderous look, during Emit Wright's funeral.

Cole and his animals had crossed five or six feeder streams during the day and as night was starting to fall, they came upon another. He decided this would be where he would prospect come morning. To the west, the sun showed just the top of its sphere above the distant treetops, like a child peering over a picket fence. The stream babbled and a cool breeze blew. For a moment, Cole took in the beauty of his surroundings and smiled. He had survived and found a way to keep the dream for Belinda and himself alive. As he looked down, the low sun to the west cast huge shadows to his right and he saw that Tusk's shadow looked like a giant wolf. He laughed quietly. "You do have some big wolf in you, don't you, boy?" Tusk cocked his head questioningly.

...

In the morning, Cole felt rejuvenated and motivated for the task ahead. As usual, his twine snares were empty, and his fishnet was holding a nice trout. He took out the fish, gutted it, and reset the net. He cooked it up in his new frying pan and ate his fill, giving Tusk a share for breakfast. By the time he returned to the water, the net had another fish. A good omen.

The day went by, like most days he had been in the Oregon Territory, with thousands of bends, scoops, and swirls. Cole called to Tusk at the water's edge. "I guess the problem wasn't Joseph's gold pan, since this new one isn't finding any gold either." He bent and scooped again. At day's end, he had three fish in reserve but no sign of gold. He moved camp upstream and settled in for the night, wondering how many more nights he would be here before he found what he was after and could turn toward home.

July 1851 – North of Salem, Oregon Territory

*I*t had been three months since his night in Salem, and Cole had never returned, determined to stay away; stay safe, until he found gold. Each passing day made him less sure there was gold in Oregon Territory. He spoke to the animals a lot now, in his solitude, though he told himself he was not going mad, he just did it to pass the time.

It was sometime in July, Cole kept marking sticks but as long as it had been, he knew he was likely off a little. It was light out, but he still lay under his tent. His bones ached all over and his joints felt creaky. He felt old at just eighteen. He could barely stand the thought of eating a fish anymore. He appreciated the abundance he had caught, as it sustained him, but the taste, which was once something he enjoyed, now nauseated him. Stepping into the water, and dipping his pan, just to look at it full of sand and rocks and water with no gold for what felt like the millionth time, he called to the animals, "Maybe we should've gone to California boys. There's no damned gold here, or it's so hidden I'll never find it. You two must think you hitched up with the wrong man, living out here in the woods, walking in water all day every day, eating nothing but goddamn fish."

Then his voice lowered, and he spoke to himself. "I've let her down. I spent all this time away, time I could've been there to help her, and it's all been for nothing. When I get back, if I even make it back, it'll all be lost." He broke down crying and it burst like a dam. Tears streamed down his face, and he held his head in his hands. Tusk climbed into his lap, looking scared and confused.

An hour later, he finally got to his feet and stumbled to where he had strung fish up in a tree with twine. He took down a fish, threw it to Tusk to eat raw, then brought Little Boy to the water to drink. He trudged back to the camp, barely lifting his feet as he scuffed through the dirt and grabbed the gold pan again. He would work on.

It was a full-sun day with punishing heat. He worked shirtless, slowly bending, scooping, swirling, dumping. He had learned that on days with full sun, white rocks or other minerals would sometimes gleam, so he no longer had a start of excitement with each sparkle. He was not even sure he'd be excited by gold right now.

Cole worked straight through lunch and began to feel light-headed and weak. He had not eaten all day and was working in the hot sun. By the look of the sun, it was midafternoon. Cole felt a cool breeze but realized he could see nothing, then he felt a cold splash and heard a thump against his head. The water revived him, and he sat up, realizing after a few moments that he had passed out like he had in the snow when he was still traveling with Phoebe and her children. He dragged himself to his feet and staggered up the embankment from the stream to his camp. The day was over early. He started to prepare a fire to eat yet another fish.

...

The next morning Cole awoke with Tusk lapping the right side of his head. He put his hand there and felt the dried blood from his fall in the creek. He sat up, groaned with the aches in his back and knees as he stood, then went to restart the evening fire so he could cook breakfast.

It was another hot day with full sun. He grabbed the gold pan and went to work after eating and caring for the animals' needs. The water was narrowing, he would need to seek a new stream within a day or two. He had moved through a dozen feeder streams at this point, since his stay in Salem. He estimated he was a good forty miles from Salem now, as he kept working north. He had not seen a single soul on two legs in more than ninety days.

The morning dragged on slowly: bend, scoop, swirl, stare, dump, and do it over again. By the time the sun was straight overhead, he felt himself stagger and knew he should eat some fish and drink some water. Cole looked up and saw a sky so blue it could almost have been compared to Belinda's eyes. There was not a single cloud. The line of trees on each side of the narrowing creek blocked all but the thick blue stripe of sky in a line that squiggled like the stream itself. It could have been a winding country road of sheer blue. It was getting harder to appreciate the good moments like this, the beauty of this place, but he tried.

A second fish was cooked at breakfast to prepare for a midday meal and allow for more time to work, though time didn't seem to matter. Trudging back into the water after a half hour to eat and rest, Cole resumed his monotony. "You know, Tusk, I learned in school years ago about Greek mythology. There was a guy who had to push a rock uphill for eternity. Another guy was chained and had his liver eaten every day by an eagle, over and over." He paused, then bent for a scoop. "Those were punishments. I wonder what I'm being punished for."

At nightfall, Cole looked up through the trees, before going under his tent. The stars were brilliant and encircled by the trees. One of the stars glowed golden, with a soft, yellow hue, versus the stark white of the others. "There you are," he said to himself and went under his tent.

The next morning, Cole went through all of his routines by rote. By the time he stood in the water, gold pan in hand, he could barely remember how he'd gotten there. He just bent and scooped. It was the third day of hot, full sun. There was less breeze today and the heat became stifling by late morning. He stripped to his undershorts and kept scooping.

Midday meal came and went, and he resumed his habitual work. Everything had become joyless. Cole looked at the dwindling stream and decided he would move on in the morning. The sun was setting and cast stripes of light across the landscape. Months earlier, he would have found beauty in the moment, but he just kept scooping.

A glint caught his eye. His heart did not jump, as he knew too well that it was likely some mineral or even a white stone.

He examined the pan more closely and saw that the stone that glinted looked gold in color, the smallest of flecks within a rock. He fought to push down hope. He knew hope as an enemy now. If he dared to hope and then saw this glint for what it was; a fraud, a deception, then he would be crushed. But as he stared, hope crept past his defenses. This looked different than anything he had seen. It looked like what Joseph Mills held in Cold Spring almost a year ago.

Cole examined every rock, pebble, and grain of sand in his pan before discarding any. Only the one rock, but it looked like what he had been seeking. His heart was pounding so hard it felt like someone hammering his ribs from inside, trying to escape.

He pocketed the rock and scooped more creek bed around where he stood. Nothing on the first scoop, so he scooped again, and again. The light was fading but there was another glint; two in fact. One was smaller than the first rock, just a spot of gold color the size of a pinhead in a small rock. The other was larger, a stripe of gold metal in a rock the size of a fingernail.

Losing light, Cole marked the spot with a stake in the creek bed and also placed rocks on the shore in a straight line pointing to the spot where he stood. He could barely say the word for fear that it would disappear and be a dream—gold.

July 1851 – Cold Spring, New York

The sun shone brightly on an early July morning. The crops were thriving after a wet spring and the warm start to summer. Belinda looked out with satisfaction at the green fields. A soft breeze brought the fragrance of wheat and corn to her. This was pure beauty and she had done this. She appreciated the hard work her mother, sister, and brother had done and knew she was not alone in the success, but she had pride in having orchestrated it. She was the head of an efficient, yet still poor, family farm. Something about the green growth; the plants swaying in a gentle breeze; the steady work of her family at her direction, all made her feel whole.

Alice and Buck were weeding the wheat fields. Mama was tending to the vegetables; harvesting what was ready to eat, scanning for bugs and pests, weeding and thinning plants. Belinda had mucked out the barn and would go take in eggs from the chickens shortly. She was at peace and felt a sense of order and calm in her new life. She still thought of Cole every day but had decided months ago to focus on what she could control. Her mother had helped her with that.

After pulling her siblings from school, working the farm six days per week, and providing schooling two hours each night for both of them, Belinda had broken down. It was early May and Mama found Belinda sobbing in her bed.

"It's not enough," Belinda said when Mama put a hand on her back. "It's never enough. Even paying the banknote; it's all interest and we don't get ahead—and work on the farm never stops—and Alice and Buck don't go to school—and they're just kids—and Cole …" She had been ranting in a hyperventilated cadence and stopped short at his name.

Mama patted her head, saying, "Oh, my girl—my beautiful girl. I just can't believe you're mine 'cuz you are so much more than I ever was. Look at what you've done, for all of us. I think maybe the only thing you can't control is Cole comin' back and that's what's got you worked up." She paused. "I'm not sayin' don't miss him but maybe you should think about all the good you've done and enjoy it a little."

It was simple but Belinda needed to hear it. There were still days that sadness gripped her, but those were fewer, and she decided to focus on the good things around her. She had a family now, such as she had never had in her life.

Belinda was jarred out of her reflection by the sound of approaching footsteps. It was Elizabeth Thomas. "Ma," Belinda said, startled, and it came out like a question. She knew that Ma had not set foot on that property since her best friend, Meg Leary, had taken her life there after losing her children. Something must have happened. Her mind raced, and she immediately worried about little Eleanor.

"Hello, dear." Ma addressed Belinda, but her eyes were locked on the barn where the Learys had ended their lives with a shotgun. She shook her head and looked directly at Belinda, with a level gaze. "When Dale came to the farm this morning ..." She paused and shook her head slightly. "Well, he saw Tommy in town last night and I thought you should know."

A chill went through Belinda's body, her face went white, and her knees shook and gave way slightly. She placed a hand on the fence that contained the chickens to steady herself. Minutes earlier she was gazing proudly upon her farm and smelling the sweet air, reflecting on the sense of order in her life, now that life felt fragile and insecure.

"Thank you for telling me. I know it wasn't easy coming here," Belinda said, trying to sound and look more composed than she felt.

Elizabeth straightened her back and gave a dismissive wave of her hand. "It's just a place and I'm long overdue here. I wish I came for a better cause." She paused, looking worried. "What can I do for you, dear?"

Belinda shook her head almost imperceptibly. "This is my burden, and you have done so much already." Both women reflected back to the standoff at the Thomas farm; Ma holding a rifle pointed at Tommy and driving him away. "I suppose I knew this day would come, though I hoped otherwise."

"Do you still have my rifle handy?"

Belinda nodded. "I keep it by the bed—loaded."

"Would you like Dale to stay here a few days? Seems having a man here could help."

"No. He has Katherine and Eleanore to look after. This is mine to deal with. Maybe he's just passing through. He hasn't been to this farm in a year. We'll be alright."

. . .

At Dinner that night, Belinda was distracted and quiet. Her mother noticed first and then Alice. Buck didn't seem to pay attention as he excitedly told a story about a burrow of rabbits he had discovered in the wheat field that had five kits in it. Belinda had been debating whether to tell the others.

"What's wrong, Bellie?" Alice broke in, using a nickname she had become fond of calling her big sister.

After a long pause, she straightened her back and tried to look as sure and confident as possible, saying, "Tommy's back."

Mama gasped and Alice let out a loud "no" in an almost involuntary shout. Buck looked around the room at the rest of his family and began to cry, more in reaction to their fear than his own. Tommy had never directly injured any of them, other than Belinda, but they all knew what this meant for the harmony and progress they had built together.

Alice spoke first. "Will you leave us? I couldn't blame you if you did."

Belinda shook her head instantly, even though until that moment she had not actually decided whether to stay or go. Hearing it out loud from her sister, who looked up to her as the head of this family, it was clear. "I'm not going anywhere." She steadied her hands, and then her gaze, looking at each of them in turn, "We are a family. We will stay together. We will bring in the wheat and corn, and we will pay that banknote again this year. No one is taking our farm, and no one is making me leave it."

Her speech seemed to convince them, if not herself, fully, though Maye looked deeply worried still. She finally spoke. "Keep the rifle handy." She paused, adding, "and don't you hesitate to use it." A tear rolled down her face.

Belinda grasped her mother's hand, wondering how hard it must have been to give permission to kill her firstborn child. A mother's love being torn in two.

After dinner, they sat in silence. Buck played with jacks and a ball on the floor, practicing how many he could pick up while still catching the ball on one bounce. At one point, Alice grabbed his hands and stopped him, and they all listened. If they had heard something outside, they were no longer sure. They were all on edge. The front door had been barred from the inside since after dinner but they still felt unsafe, unsure. Buck fell asleep on the floor, then they all decided to turn in. Allice carried him to bed and the rest headed off for what would be a fitful night's rest.

The morning came and light streamed into the windows. The sound of birds chirping and the chickens clucking made for a normal feeling of the farm life they had enjoyed up until Elizabeth Thomas's visit the prior day. Belinda began to wonder, or perhaps it was hope, whether Tommy was really interested in any of them anymore. He had moved on a year ago. He could have been in town for anything.

Belinda unbarred the door, holding the rifle, and the family gathered behind her as she opened it, half expecting Tommy's hulking figure to be standing there, blocking the light from the doorway like an eclipse. A soft breeze and sunlight were all that came bursting into the house. Belinda walked out and started her chores, turning back to the house to direct her family. "The morning chores won't do themselves, let's get a move on."

It was a perfect morning in the Hudson Valley. July tended to have hot days, but the nights still cooled into the fifties. It was just an hour after sunup and the air was still crisp under a brilliant blue sky. Belinda entered the barn, walked past one empty horse stall, then opened the second stall that housed their plow horse, Scotty. They had never had the funds for a second horse but hoped to fill that stall when the farm was paid off and funds were not all drained by the banknote. Scotty was a strong, all-black horse with a good temperament. Belinda led Scotty from his pen into the open space of the barn and used the pitchfork to spear and pile some hay for him while she mucked out the pen. Then she went to gather eggs for breakfast. The day felt normal; unremarkable.

During the afternoon Belinda joined her mother tending the large vegetable garden. The tomatoes were coming in nicely, though not yet ripe. Tommy's presence was slipping to the back of her mind with the nearby rifle providing the occasional reminder. The two women worked well together and had become so much closer over the past months. There was a sound in the wooded area beyond the barn and they both wheeled around and froze, staring. Belinda slowly reached for the rifle and lifted it.

They both held their positions for what seemed like an eternity but was actually only a few minutes. There was no more sound.

That night was uneventful as well, as were the following day and night. Perhaps Tommy truly had moved on from his hatred and anger. Perhaps it was a coincidence that he passed through town, and he had no intention of visiting the farm.

A week passed and life on the farm returned to normal. There was so much work to do and little time to worry about anything else. Sheathing and bundling wheat was grueling work for large men and they were a group comprised of an older woman, a younger woman, and two children. It had been an especially long day, as they made the final push to finish the wheat harvest for the year.

Maye and Belinda cleaned up after a late dinner. The exhausted family went to their beds without much conversation. Maye checked that the door was barred and went to change into her nightdress. Belinda didn't even change, exhausted, she threw herself onto her mattress and was asleep within moments.

A rattling sound woke Belinda from a deep sleep. At first, she could hardly place where she was, never mind the origin of the sound. Coming to her senses slowly, she realized it was the front door. Someone, or some animal, was trying to get in. The sound stopped and she waited, frozen with fear. "Mama?" She whispered.

"I heard it," came back to her in a whisper through the thin wall to the next room. Belinda looked at Alice and Buck—both were still asleep; Alice face down, a tangle of hair obscuring her face; Buck on his back, mouth wide open, breathing loudly.

Belinda glanced up at the window, where a pale moonlight shone into the room. It was too small for Tommy to fit through, not much more than a foot across. Mama had joined her in the room now and huddled close by. They both knew they shared the same thoughts. Tommy was here, but everything was quiet. There was a sudden and thunderous crack at the front door, causing the children to wake and scream. It was followed by a creak and then another crack with the sound of splintering wood. It was unmistakable—he had an axe and was chopping through the door.

The four of them huddled on one mattress now. Buck and Alice were sobbing. Maye grabbed Belinda by both cheeks and stared into her eyes, which were a dark midnight blue color in the pale moonlight from the window, and said, "Use the rifle." She motioned her head toward the door.

Belinda looked at Alice and Buck, grabbed the rifle, then shook her head. "He could have a gun too; or what if the bullet doesn't stop him? I'm not putting you all in the middle of a shootout. He's come for me and me alone."

"But what else can you …" Maye started to ask, then trailed off when she followed Belinda's gaze to the window and knew what her daughter was thinking.

Belinda nodded, seeing the flash of understanding in her mother's eyes. "I'm going to draw him away from the house." Belinda grabbed the rifle, which was leaning against the wall near her mattress, and went swiftly, but quietly toward the window.

There was another thunderous crash at the door. He would be in soon. She threw up the sash, handed her mother the rifle, and shimmied through the narrow opening headfirst. As she fell, she hit the ground, bracing with her hands, and felt a snap and a burst of pain in her right hand. She muffled a scream by covering her mouth with her left hand. Her mother handed the rifle out the window and Belinda ran toward the barn, carrying it in her left hand. As she reached the barn, she yelled through the pale, moonlit darkness, "Over here," and ran inside.

The hacking sounds stopped, replaced by the sound of heavy, running footsteps coming toward the barn. Belinda slipped through the barn quietly and opened the gate to the empty pen next to Scotty's. The black horse looked zebra striped by the thin horizontal bars of pale moonlight that shone in between the gaps in the plankboard barn walls. He let out a snort, having been disrupted from sleep. She slid to the far side of the pen with her back against the wall, holding the rifle steady with her left hand, then tried to bring her right hand to the trigger, but she could not move it.

Tommy burst into the barn, huffing from swinging a heavy axe and then sprinting with it to the barn. "Where are you, you little bitch?" She could hear him casting about with his axe. It struck the pen next to her and Scotty let out a frightened snort and shuffled his feet. "I'm head of this family, not you ... you uppity little shit." His speech was slow and slurred, obviously from drink. "I hate you ... you and your piece of shit daddy ... and you're gonna join him soon ... where are you?"

There was rustling in the hay, as he chopped his axe down,

hoping she was hiding in the pile. Then he went quiet. Belinda held her breath, hoping he couldn't hear her in her panic. The razor-thin strips of pale light coming between the barn boards revealed the pen door opening slowly, but she saw nothing of Tommy's shape yet. Then he stepped in and loomed in front of her. She raised the rifle, aimed it at the center of his massive shadowy figure, forced her lame hand to the trigger, and pulled with all her might. Nothing happened. Her brain told her hand to contract around the trigger, but the hand did not respond. She had no feeling in it and her heart sank, watching her fate unfold before her.

Belinda closed her eyes and dropped the rifle. She whispered softly, "Cole."

Tommy lifted the axe above his head. A beam of light shone across the blade as he began to bring it down.

July 1851 – North of Salem, Oregon Territory

Cole couldn't sleep as he lay out under the stars. It was a clear warm night in early July, and he wanted to experience every sense of it, on what had been a momentous day. His small fire crackled and gave off a smoky pine scent. Little Boy, whom he kept on a long lead at night, wandered around, creating a muffled hoof-beat sound on the pine-needle-covered ground. With his eyes closed, it sounded like the shuffling of cards. Staring straight up, the trees reluctantly revealed patches of sky that were littered with brilliant stars. The trees swayed in a gentle breeze that had picked up after sunset. The air was cooling quickly.

Every few moments, Cole would remove the three pebbles from his pocket and confirm they were really there. He knew he still had a lot of work to do but vowed to enjoy this moment. He thought back to his journey and how long it had taken him; about the moments when he felt like giving up. He thought about his hunger on the road west, the countless crosses, wondering if he would be one more who died on the road. He thought about discovering his supplies had been stolen and not knowing if he could continue to prospect. He thought about the pure monotony and discouragement of the past three months.

Cole shook his head and sighed. Even thinking back to the challenges, he was serene now. His mind turned to the people who had been kind to him. It started with Joseph Mills, who was generous with his knowledge and equipment. The toll man at the Allegheny River bridge and Priscilla, known as Missy, in Pittsburgh, gave him useful warnings. Even the meek innkeeper, John, in Salem, who likely had to steel his nerves in order to come to the table as Lev and Burl were on the edge of violence. Of course, he thought most about the Ryerson family, who he met by chance or some design, and spent the winter with, traveling the harsh road from Independence, Missouri all the way to Salem, Oregon. Cyrus, who had left on his mission knowing he may well die before arrival. Two children who lost their father and endured more hunger and pain than he had known possible when he was their age. And Phoebe, the latest of three powerful women who had shaped his life.

He drifted asleep and slept more soundly than he had in months.

He sprang awake as if jolted. His campsite was peaceful, and the animals were calm. The embers of his fire were faintly visible, looking warm but not hot. The air was crisp, in sharp contrast to the heat of the prior days. It sharpened his senses and he remembered why he woke; it was his dream. He never remembered dreams, but this one was vivid. Belinda had leaned over him at this very campsite and beckoned him home.

It felt so real that he felt sadness that she had gone so quickly. He wished he had stayed in that state to hold her, speak with her. He had heard her voice in that moment, felt her breath and her warmth. She was there, if only for a moment.

. . .

Morning came and Cole was surprised to have fallen back to sleep at all. His dream was still clear in his mind. He had been called home and needed to work quickly to locate the source of the gold filtering down into the creek bed, break it free, bring it to Tom in Salem, then head home. It would take many months to get home, but he was eager to start.

After rushing through his breakfast routine, he walked down to the creek and waded in to resume his search. Cole recalled Joseph Mills's instructions for locating the source. He had said, "You keep panning, steadily upstream. You should find more and more, then suddenly nothin'. That's when you look up the hill on the side where the most gold was and start pokin' and diggin' 'til you find the deposit." It sounded easy, but nothing on this journey had felt as easy as he once thought it might be. Cole would not underestimate the challenge.

It was a cooler, overcast day, the weather having changed overnight. Cole located the line of rocks he had placed on the bank about two hundred yards upstream from his camp. He was glad he had laid those out because the stake in the water had washed away. His first few scoops yielded nothing, and he began to fear it was all a dream; there was no gold. But within the first thirty minutes, he found another small rock with gold flecks. He pocketed the rock and moved on; there was no time to celebrate; he had a mission to get on the road home.

As Cole moved slowly upstream, the frequency of gold-flecked rocks increased. By mid-morning almost every scoop had signs of gold and he grew more and more excited and confident. His pockets became too full just before noontime and he made a small pile on the bank. There would be no break today; no midday meal. His spirits were high and there was too much excitement to stop now. At first, he was finding the rocks randomly across the stream, from the left bank where his camp sat to the right. The farther he moved upstream, the trail of gold-flecked rocks led him to the right side of the waterway. In the midafternoon, he bent and dipped his gold pan into the creek bed about two feet from the right edge. He was perhaps one hundred yards upstream from where he started the day. When he swirled the mixture of rocks, sand, and water, he saw a night sky of stars staring back at him. At least eight rocks sparkled with gold in a single scoop of his pan. Instinctively, he looked up the right-side incline and said aloud, "I've got you now. I know you're up there."

Taking another few steps upstream Cole scooped and swirled and as he expected, there was nothing; a starless sky. He stepped back to the spot where the concentration was greatest and placed a marker in stones on the right bank. As he stared up the slope, he scanned for any obvious signs of his treasure but saw none. The ground sloped gently up from the stream and became lightly wooded with pines about ten feet from the water, with the trees becoming gradually denser up the slope. There appeared to be a slight dip in the land, starting fifty feet from the water and running up the slope. This, Cole decided, was where he would start to look.

It would be important to map out the area so as to avoid duplicating the search. Cole started to create a visual grid, using trees. He took out his small knife and made a mark on the tree closest to the water and about ten feet to the right of where the gold deposit started. He did the same with a tree to the left and then began to scour the ground between them. The work was painstaking because the gold was likely being deposited through an underground spring, but it was up here, of that he was certain. On his hands and knees, Cole combed through the pine needles and underbrush with his hands and then poked the ground with a stick, seeking softer spots where there could be water underneath.

After he had covered about ten feet up past the two trees he had marked, he marked two more trees so that the square made by the four marked trees behind him represented an area that had been searched. Returning to his hands and knees he scoured the next section of ground working his way up, away from the water. Occasionally, Tusk came by and sniffed the ground, wondering what was so interesting. The work went on for hours and the light gave way to dusk, making the search impossible.

Cole looked up to the sky, and said aloud, "I'm sorry, Blue. I wanted to leave in the morning, but it looks like I have another day here." The dream flooded back to him—she had called him home. As far as he had come and as close as he was to their goal, he still felt a strong tug to abandon the gold and just go back to her now. He committed to one more day, but he would have to leave soon.

The collection of small rocks from the creek bed was impressive when viewed together. Cole stared at the glittering pile as he cooked up two fish for dinner. There were more than fifty glinting, glowing stones. As the fire crackled the light danced off the stones piled a few feet away creating almost a mirror image of the fire. "I wonder what they are worth, boys," Cole asked the animals rhetorically. He knew most had not more than a speck of gold, but a dozen or so had thick lines of gold striped across them. "There must be an ounce at least, but we didn't come all this way and live out here like this for twenty dollars, did we, boys?"

That night Cole slept soundly and woke before dawn. He fed and watered Little Boy and had breakfast before sunup. As soon as daylight broke, he was on the far slope. It was another cooler, overcast morning, perfect for working. A low-lying mist hung over the slope, thickening about fifty feet up. When standing in the creek, where the air was perfectly clear, and looking up at the mist hanging above, it looked as if a white sheet was billowing above him. Cole mused that the hills were using the mist to hide the gold from him.

He returned to his grid and kept working up the slope. He had reached the area where the ground was cleft, and he focused hard on the areas of depression. Section after section he moved his way up the slope, poking with a stick, moving rocks, and digging with his hands.

It was before just noontime, the mist had lifted, and the light was good, in spite of the cloud cover. Cole was combing carefully through every contour of the ground, lifting and examining each rock. Tusk was up the slope from him looking down and cocking his head from side to side. "What do you see, boy?" Cole moved up by the dog who was staring at the ground, which looked unremarkable to Cole, though slightly concave. He spoke to his dog again. "It's not what you *see*, is it, boy? That's how you look when you hear something." He put his ear to the ground and heard running water.

Taking a stick and prodding the ground, it penetrated and was wet when he withdrew it. The hammer pounded inside Cole's chest yet again. Using the stick, Cole carved into the ground and eventually stirred it into mud, which he mucked out with both hands. He was on all fours, pulling the mud out and flinging it backward between his legs, as an animal would dig a hole. Then his hands hit flowing water about a foot below the surface and dirt caved in around the hole. Cole let his hands explore the trickling water and felt rock just below the surface, the water of this underground spring ran only inches deep and perhaps a foot wide, carrying water from the hills down to the creek, which in turn fed the Willamette River. He reflected on the marvel of how the earth operates, all pieces working, flowing together.

There was no way to break the rock free and look at it above the surface. It was a large continuous piece, made smooth by years of water running over it. He would have to excavate more dirt and allow the light to penetrate the water in order to see what was there. It could well be granite or some other rock deposit unrelated to the gold in the creek, but Cole felt more confident than ever that he had found what he came three thousand miles for; what he had risked everything for.

With no pickaxe, the work was tedious. He marked a circle about six feet in diameter and dug with a sharp stick and then his hands. It took the better part of an hour to remove about six inches of rocky soil from the full circle. He then focused on the areas above the flowing water. With the rocky surface removed, the work went more quickly, aided by the water itself helping to wash away the dirt as he cleared it. He thought, *The hill is giving up now. It knows I've won.*

Cole stood over the hole he had created. The rock below the water's surface now had a glow. A small beam of sunlight peered through the cloud cover for the first time all day and Cole saw, through the clear, babbling spring water, gray rock with thick strips of gold metal running horizontally through it. Tears welled in his eyes, and he fell onto his backside and sat, staring at his find. This time he did not think of the journey, nor of the hardships, he thought only of his Belinda. He had not seen her in ten months, but his love felt stronger than ever. He hoped she was feeling the same way. He was about to head home.

Cole rocked forward and got to his knees, placing both hands into the water to feel the rock. He worked his fingers along the surface but found no end. He walked a short distance and found a sturdy branch to wedge in and hopefully move or chip off the rock. When he tried, the stick broke and the realization struck him that this was immovable without a pickaxe. The reality hit him hard and stung, feeling like a starving man who found food but then realized it was just out of reach. He would now have to trek to Salem for a pickaxe and return here; forty miles each way. With no saddle, he couldn't even ride Little Boy to hasten the pace.

He considered the idea of leaving the gold behind and just heading home. Belinda had called him home; she needed him. He knew, though, that he had to complete his mission, being this close. He would just have to make up time on the journey east and go without sleep if necessary.

There was no time to think about the path forward. He had to leave now and make half the trip to Salem tonight so he could complete it tomorrow before the general store closed. He could not waste a day before heading home. Cole called to Tusk, "We are headed to town, boy," and went to pack up his camp and lead his animals through most of the night.

Cole placed markers showing the path to his find, for when he returned, but in truth, he felt as if he could find this spot blindfolded now. He packed up camp in a few minutes and headed west toward the Willamette River, he would then turn south and trek about forty miles to town. Before leaving camp, he buried and marked the gold rocks he had taken from the river. It would be too dangerous to carry those into town and risk being followed back to his find.

The travel felt brisk and easy, even as night fell. Cole no longer felt old, tired, and weak. He felt that he could do anything, and he was driven to get home to Belinda. By the time they reached the Willamette, it was dusk, and the river looked black in the fading light. Cole led Little Boy and occasionally stroked his head while Tusk trotted along in front of them.

When night had fallen fully, Tusk looked up at Cole and gave a few plaintive whines, reminding him that this was the time they slept. But they trudged on. Sometime in the early morning hours, Cole relented and stopped to sleep. He did not unpack anything, instead just laying down under a tree to close his eyes for a bit. He woke after perhaps an hour. He and Tusk ate some cooked fish he had packed in his rucksack. He had gotten into the habit of cooking two or three meals at a time since he did not need a fire every night for warmth at this time of year.

Morning light came soon after they had set out again. Cole estimated they could cover the remaining distance and reach town in the afternoon, well before the store would close. He had resolved to leave town immediately after he bought his pickaxe and sleep during the trek back to his camp, where unwelcome eyes would not be on him.

It was a beautiful day to travel, with moderate temperature and a light drizzle that barely got them wet and didn't even soak through a layer of clothes. A breeze blew ripples into the surface of the river, making it opaque. The trees swayed gently while the wind seemed to be whispering an unknown message through the pine needles.

It appeared to be late afternoon when Cole saw the town ahead along the east bank of the river. He would be approaching from the end where the refinery sat, though he had no intention of going there and arousing suspicion. He would have to get to the other side of town where the general store was situated. He decided to tether Little Boy here and walk in only with Tusk. He walked the horse about fifty feet into the woods and gave him a long lead tied to a tree.

The town was bustling. As he passed the refinery, Cole saw a few people outside with rucksacks or saddlebags. It looked like he may not have been the only one to make a find. He saw all of the familiar sights from the saloon to the brothel and approached the farther end of town where the inn stood to his right and the general store to his left. He turned inside and Tusk knew to wait out front.

At the counter, a potbellied man of about fifty sat on a high stool, so it almost looked like he was standing. He had hair that looked like it was once black, but gray had taken over the majority of his head and all of his beard. He wore a smock and his round face bore a gentle smile. "Good afternoon," he welcomed.

"Hello, I'd like a pickaxe please," Cole said in a friendly but brisk manner. He was intent on making this a short stay in town.

"Oh, had some luck, have we?" The man smiled.

"No, just want to be prepared. I'm an optimist." Cole smiled broadly, causing his dark eyes to narrow to slits.

"Well, that's the way to be. I've got the large ones in back for three dollars and over here the smaller ones are two." He pointed to a shelf with three pickaxes, all about the size of the one Joseph Mills had given Cole that was later stolen.

Wanting to be less conspicuous as he left town, the smaller ones seemed fine. He picked up one of them, felt the heft and balance, then nodded. He removed his last two dollars from his sack and placed them on the counter. Noticing the jerky for sale, he decided a break from fish was worth spending the last of his smaller coins.

"Good luck to you, young man," the shopkeeper said, adding a wave of his hand.

Cole had a twinge of regret that he was being so secretive. There were good people in the world, and it was a shame that the few bad ones made him so untrusting. He walked from the shop smiling, with the pickaxe over his shoulder and his eyes met Burl's across the road. He was headed to the tavern and had looked straight across at Cole. Lev was not with him, and Cole hoped that he had not recognized him. Burl was not bright and may not have registered Cole's face at all. Nonetheless, he was eager to leave town. He called to Tusk and walked briskly down the road, past the refinery and along the river, glancing back every hundred yards or so. He saw no one in pursuit.

They reached Little Boy and Cole untethered him, led him back to the river, and turned north. He was excited to return to his work and then head home as soon as possible, having completed his mission. He did not feel tired, despite the lack of sleep, but realistically, he knew he could not travel forty miles back to camp with no sleep. He decided to trek for a few hours, just to put some distance between them and Salem, and then set camp and sleep at least a quarter mile into the woods away from the river.

Cole took his animals north along the river until nightfall, then turned east and traveled another ten minutes, finding a nice clearing with some grass for his horse. He laid down and slept almost instantly. He woke with a start, just before daybreak.

He wondered if he had been dreaming again but could not remember anything. Then he heard Tusk give a low growl. He was looking south through the trees, but Cole could see nothing in the faint glow of the pre-sunrise morning. He wondered if a bear was lurking but felt safe with Tusk there to chase him off. Black bears were skittish, as he had seen before.

Awake now, Cole decided to head out. They trekked back to the waterside and turned north again. He ate some jerky along the way, which was a welcome respite from fish. He shared some with Tusk, telling the dog, "This won't last long, boy, so we still will need some fish. We'll find a good stream on the way back." At midday they came upon a perfect resting spot by a stream, flowing east to west into the Willamette River. It would likely have fish and there was lush, tall grass for Little Boy to graze on. Cole set his net, but he also wanted to hunt more directly, as they did not have time to await the whims of the fish. He snapped off a forked branch from a sapling and removed the leaves and excess length, so he was left with a stick about a quarter inch in diameter, eighteen inches long with a right and left fork at the end, each being about two inches. The idea was to pin a fish to the bottom in shallow water where they could not maneuver as well. He had done this with Dale back in New York in his youth.

Stepping out in the stream, Cole looked for fish. Within a few minutes, a trout swam by. It bypassed the net Cole had set and also stuck to deeper water where Cole would not be able to use his makeshift tool. It was about ten minutes before the next fish came and it was a fat trout. It bypassed the net but swam over the shallow, rocky creek bed. Cole struck quickly, missing his mark slightly as he aimed for the fat center of the fish, but he still pinned its head down and was able to grasp the body tightly with his left hand and toss it ashore. He started a fire and cooked up the fish for later. While it was cooking, the net snared another one, so they had two meals in reserve.

They hiked late into the evening, with the late summer sunlight helping their cause. They had made enough progress so that they could realistically get back to the gold before noon the next day. Cole hoped to get the gold out and head back to Salem a day later. He felt every hour of delay as a betrayal to Belinda's plea for him to come home. He knew it was a dream, but believed it meant more.

The following morning, they got on their way at dawn. Tusk had growled again during the night but then settled back down. Just before noon, they arrived back at the camp. It was undisturbed. Cole tethered his horse and headed over to the gold deposit with his pickaxe slung over his shoulder. After ten months away from home, tomorrow he would head east and spend every day of his life with the woman he loved. He would secure their future and the future of her whole family.

After surveying the rock with his hands again, Cole started clearing more dirt from the area and exposing the rock more fully. The work with the pickaxe was faster and smoother than digging with a stick and his hands. He gouged the hard soil with the sharp point of the axe, creating an outline of where he wanted to clear the soil. Then he softened the packed ground inside the marked area with smooth, easy strokes. He could remove the soil by hand then and expose more of the rock.

As the rock revealed itself, it looked like a sunrise, glowing with a small glimmer at first and then bursting into full daylight as it rose. Cole stared in awe at the huge veins of gold running through a section of rock that was several feet long and more than a foot wide. He could never remove and carry the entire rock, but he felt sure he could chip around the veining and remove the section that was mostly gold, which was perhaps four inches wide and over a foot long. He decided to start driving the point of the axe several inches from the gold.

Kneeling by the opening in the ground, water soaked through Cole's jeans. He raised the axe about two feet above the rock and brought it down cautiously. It made a spark and clanged loudly, causing Tusk to jump up and run twenty feet down the slope. Cole laughed. "You chase bears but run from loud noises—crazy dog."

The axe barely made a mark in the stone, so Cole raised it over his head and brought it down harder. A small chip flew off to the side and more sparks flew. He repeated the action, slowly chipping the stone. On one strike, he came down on the edge of the gold veining and the tip of the pickaxe sunk into the soft metal. He adjusted his knees to help aim farther from the gold and struck the stone again and again. An hour into the effort, Cole had made a line of chips, some deep, about three inches away from the large gold vein. Aiming for a deeply chipped spot, he brought the axe down hard, hitting his mark, and he heard a loud, splintering crack. A fissure in the rock had opened, wide enough to wedge in the point of the pickaxe.

The axe tip fit about two inches into the crack. The axe handle hovered horizontally over the ground. Cole stood, knees bent, straddling the handle and grasping it firmly with both hands. He jerked up sharply, using his legs and all of his strength. The crack widened. He repeated the same motion, now with one side of the pickaxe head all the way down in the crack and the handle laying against the ground. He bent low and jerked up, the section of rock shifted but the axe handle cracked and separated from the head.

Cole dropped to his knees and tossed the broken pickaxe aside. He grasped the rock with both and shook it—it moved. He worked it forward and back and felt it loosen in the soil. After just a few minutes, he was able to dig his arms deep into the wet soil around the rock and find the lower edge with his fingers. Lifting the section of broken stone was more awkward than heavy. The sheared piece was perhaps ten pounds. He was able to heft the section out of the mucky dirt and drag it to the flat surface.

Picking up the jagged rock under one arm and holding the pickaxe head in his other hand, Cole walked to the creek and placed it in the water, letting the flowing water wash it clean. It sparkled brilliantly.

It was evening but the sun was still up in the long days of summer. Cole looked up the slope. His broken axe handle lay by the hole. A hole that undoubtedly had a lot more treasure to reveal. He was done though. His life, his treasure, was in Cold

Spring, New York. He had accomplished what he set out to do. With the value of this rock, the farm would be safe, and he would live his life there with Belinda and her family. He picked up the ten-pound rock, that was perhaps as much as one-quarter pure gold, and walked away without looking back again.

Back at the camp, that they had left days before, Cole prepared for a final night and looked around with fondness at the ratty little camp area he'd made. It was the closest thing to a home he'd had since leaving Cold Spring. He'd almost given up here; he'd had his dream of Belinda here; he'd found gold flecks in the water here; and he'd found the rock that would save Belinda's farm and family here.

Tonight, Cole resolved to get a good rest and then head out at first light to trek to Salem to cash in his gold. Then he would head home. He spoke to his traveling companions. "Boys, we did it, and I couldn't have made it without you both." He held up the shining, gold-striped rock. "There's gotta be more than two pounds of pure gold in this, maybe as much as three pounds. We'll get you a saddle soon, buddy." He patted Little Boy's muzzle.

After a quiet dinner of river trout that actually tasted better knowing he was leaving, Cole lay back with his head resting on his rucksack. The gold rock laid a foot to his right. It was still light with the summer sun of the Pacific Northwest, but he was ready to rest. A serene look graced his face as he let out a sigh and let his arms fall to his side. His dog curled up a few feet away. He hoped to dream about Belinda again. His eyes closed.

Cole started awake. It was dark now and felt like it must be the middle of the night. In his fog of sleep, he wondered if this were a dream. Would he see Belinda leaning over him? As the night air roused his senses, he heard Tusk growling low and then let out a vicious flurry of barks, such as he had never heard from him, even when he chased the bear. These barks had both fear and violence in them, in equal measure. There was no fire that night, so no glow of embers to help him see, just a partial moon. A stick snapped behind him, on the east side of his camp, and he whirled around but the trees and darkness held whatever, or whoever, was there. The sound of heavy feet on pine needles came from the west side of the camp. He strained his eyes and saw a large shadowy figure. It reminded him of Tommy, and he thought of how he had wet his pants with fear—a fear like he felt now.

A voice came from the east side of camp. "Gee, still no sign of that partner." Lev emerged from the shadow of the trees with malice in his eyes and a rope in his left hand. The bear tooth on the leather rope around his neck was white in the moonlight

An answer came from the west of camp, now just a dozen feet away. "Yeah, no partner." The hulking shadow of Burl laughed at his partner's wit. Burl stepped forward revealing himself in the faint moonlight. He was holding his Jim Bowie hunting knife, its long, eight-inch silver blade giving off a soft glow.

"What do you want? H-How did you find me?" Cole hated how his voice trembled and stammered asking the questions.

"Well, we want your gold there. We saw you digging it up. Stayed downwind and at a safe distance so your dog wouldn't catch a scent." Lev smiled, "Ya know, we're in the fur trade. That means we're trackers. Darned good ones, I'd say too." His smile vanished and his voice dropped lower. "'Course we can't have you around makin' trouble for *our* gold claim." He emphasized *our*. He nodded to Burl, who lunged forward with his knife held in front of him.

Tusk leapt forward between Cole, who was frozen with fear, and the giant of a man surging forward. He sunk his teeth into Burl's left leg, just below the knee; his three long fangs sinking deep into the fleshy leg. Burl roared with pain and dropped to a knee. He gathered himself and slashed at the dog latched onto his leg, sinking the blade of his knife into Tusk's side and tearing a long gash from the dog's belly to his front leg. Tusk yelped with pain and released his grip on the leg, but with another surge, he jumped at the giant man's throat, which was now within his reach as Burl had dropped to a knee. Tusk sunk his teeth in and held tight.

Burl cried out and dropped the knife, but the cry was cut off almost instantly as the dog clenched down on his throat and violently shook his head back and forth. Burl rolled to his back, Tusk still attached to his throat, ripping at it. There was a tearing sound and a sickening gurgle, then the giant's arms went limp.

Transfixed by what was happening before him, Cole had not seen Lev sneak behind him, loop a rope over his head, and pull it tight around his neck. He flailed with his hands and grasped at the rope, but he could not pull it loose enough to take a breath. In front of him, he saw Tusk take two steps toward him and fall on his side, panting heavily, blood soaking his fur on his left side.

Cole began to lose his vision; the sight of Tusk a blur now; Burl's motionless body disappearing. It felt like a dream. He knew he had to fight for his life but could not sense direction anymore. He threw fists wildly behind his head, feeling contact more than once. He spun around but was still being strangled. Landing a blow, he felt himself falling forward. He landed on the ground with Lev on his back still, choking. His head had hit something hard, and he felt the warm sensation of blood cascading down his face. He grasped for the rope and felt what he had landed on. It was the head of his broken pickaxe.

In that moment, Cole felt a surge of anger, of fear, of love: love for Belinda, for Ma, for Dale. He saw the farm; he saw the piles of dirt with buried secrets. He saw Belinda's blazing blue eyes. He would see them again—he must. He grabbed the pickaxe head with both hands, rolled hard to his side to free his arms, and he drove it straight back by his own head, so close that he grazed his ear. As it landed, it felt like when he had hit the gold vein, rather than the rock surface, earlier that day—it sunk in. The rope went slack.

. . .

The walk to Salem was arduous and took three full days, making slow progress. The town lay ahead just a few hundred yards. Cole thought back to the night of the attack and tried to sort out what had happened and in what order. His head ached and he bore a wound five inches long down the left side of his forehead that extended into his hair. It was curved, like the pickaxe head he had landed on. His grazed ear had already scabbed over and would leave a smaller scar.

He recalled the aftermath first, stumbling around in the dark with two dead men on the ground; a badly wounded dog between them. He had taken his needle from his rucksack and pulled several long hairs from Little Boy's tail. He stitched up Tusk's side and stroked his head as he panted, eyes closed, motionless except for shallow breathing. He owed his life to this dog; the dog that was now slung over his shoulder like a nap sack, inside half of his burlap tent cover, with blood seeping through it. Tusk was breathing still, quietly but steadily. He was still hanging on.

He recalled gathering his supplies, plus the large gold-veined rock and the pile of smaller stones. He had cut the burlap tent cover in half using Burl's Jim Bowie knife, wrapped his supplies and gold in it, then loaded it all on Little Boy. Since then, he had been walking—slowly. He had considered whether the horse could carry his wounded dog but decided he couldn't take the risk of him falling off. Tusk's grip on life was too fragile. This dog gave him everything. He was Cole's burden to bear. Using the other half of the burlap cover, he wrapped the dying dog as gently as possible for the journey. He had been carrying him for three days.

They managed only seven miles on the first day. Every step felt like an accomplishment; every stream crossing, like forging a mighty river. The second day they managed almost twice as many miles, as Cole recovered his strength. Today, Cole traveled nearly twenty miles to reach Salem, motivated more with every step closer. Now, he stood just feet away.

...

The guards sat on either side of the door at the refinery. Cole seemed to remember them as larger than they looked now. They looked startled at his appearance. Cole had not seen his own face yet but knew it was blood-stained and deeply gouged, so he imagined he was a frightful sight. He laid Tusk down gently by Little Boy and removed his rucksack from the horse, which now contained his large rock and the smaller stones. He walked past the guards who just looked at each other and shrugged.

Cole strode into the refinery storefront and set the sack on the high desktop, saying, "Hello, Tom. I've brought gold."

The older man looked shocked and replied, "Good lord, son. What in the hell happened?"

"No time for that now. I have a wounded dog and need to find a doc. But I can't go carrying this around town. I trust you. I'll be back." He flipped the top of the sack open, leaving it on the desk, turned, and walked out. As he passed by the guards he heard, "Well, holy shit!" from Tom inside.

Cole turned to the guards and said in a commanding voice, "Watch my horse," then picked Tusk up gently and walked toward town. The guards sat in stunned silence.

Walking through town, Cole passed the brothel, with six women standing out on the porch. He thought that these women would know everyone and everything about what went on in town. "Ladies, I have a wounded dog here. I need a doctor or someone with medical training. Who in town do I need to see?"

A red-haired woman of about thirty years with a large bust and full hips replied. "Doc don't come here but once a week.

But Penny has helped him, and she's got some supplies, cuz a lot of what doc treats in town starts right here, if you get me." She gave a wink, adding, "Come on in."

Penny was a girl close to Cole's age with a slender build and brown curly hair in pigtails. She was a half-head shorter than Cole, with narrow hips and smaller but shapely breasts that she tried to accentuate. She wore a low-cut white linen dress and had ribbons tied in bows around her pigtails. She was soft-spoken and had kind hazel eyes. It seemed to Cole that she had been dressed to look like a much younger child. He thought to himself how strange it was that some men liked that sort of thing.

She led Cole to a bedroom and had him lay Tusk on his right side. She looked sadly at the dog, made a tsking sound with her mouth, and asked, "Poor thing, what happened?"

"He saved my life," was Cole's only reply. He had no intention of telling people about the attack.

"Well, you did good with what you had," she said, while running her hand over the horse-hair sutures. She pulled a medical supply bag from under the bed. "Doc keeps this here for when he visits." She gave a shy look to Cole, making it clear to him that the Doc visited her specifically. He must be one of those men who liked her looking like a child.

Tusk lay panting but his eyes were open. He wagged his tail looking at Cole. On his side, the blood had dried creating crusty, dark red fur that looked like a miniature mountain range. There were places where the stitching had not fully closed the skin, exposing raw flesh.

Penny took out a bottle of fluid. "This'll keep infection out.

I never did stitchin' but seen it enough times. I'll just close up where it's ragged." She proceeded to thread a small needle from the bag and pour alcohol over it. "Hold him steady." She stitched up the open areas as Tusk moaned plaintively.

As she finished, Penny looked up at Cole and reached out to touch his head. She gently felt the wound and said, "Ya know, you're not much better off than him, with that gash. I'm a little scared to try stitchin' a person but I could if you want. It's gonna leave a nasty scar either way, but it'd be best to close it up against infection."

Cole nodded.

She asked him to sit on the bed, threaded the needle, and brought it to his forehead. She leaned in so her face was just inches away, staring into the wound. There were bits of dirt in the dried blood and a flap of skin hung down just outside his hairline on the left side of his forehead. She wetted a clean cloth with the solution she had used on Tusk and dabbed his head gently. When she was satisfied it was clean, she took the threaded needle in her hand, which was shaking. Cole took her other hand and gave a slight squeeze, letting her know it was okay. As she poked the needle through the flap of skin, her face scrunched in pain as if she could feel it penetrating. After the first stitch, she looked into Cole's eyes, checking if he was alright, and he nodded. The rest of the stitching went easily.

Penny checked her work, running her fingers along the stitches, then her hand slid softly down Cole's left cheek and she looked into his eyes. She no longer looked like a child. He saw now that under the painted cheeks and childlike bows in her hair, Penny was a beautiful girl. Cole felt a sensation he had never felt with anyone but Belinda. He looked into Penny's clear hazel eyes and saw that she felt it too. She bent and kissed his right cheek softly. As her lips lingered on his skin, he could feel her breath. She moved her mouth to his, but Cole dropped his head and whispered, "I've got a girl."

Cole stood and looked down at Penny, her eyes glassy. She nodded understanding and stepped back. They wrapped the dog back up in his burlap and Cole picked the ends up holding it as if Tusk were a hammock. He nodded and smiled at Penny with pressed lips. She placed a bottle of the cleaning fluid in the burlap hammock with Tusk and instructed him to keep both of their wounds clean.

Cole turned at the door, calling back to her, "I'd like to pay you for your service."

She looked down, embarrassed, and shook her head. "That's alright, I was glad to help."

Cole smiled and said, "Doctors get paid. I'll be back with your money tomorrow." He saw a look of pride flash on her face at being called a doctor.

. . .

With Tusk in his makeshift sling, Cole headed to the inn. John, the innkeeper, was at the desk. He looked up, startled, and began to say, "What hap …"

Cole interrupted and spoke with level determination. "No time for stories right now, John. I need a room. Tusk here will be staying in the room with me, and I'll pay an extra dollar for him. You'll have the money in the morning."

John was silent, then simply motioned for Cole to follow him to a room. As he turned from the room, he spoke timidly. "I have a stable boy now, if you want to board your horse."

"I do. Thank you." Cole patted John's shoulder in thanks, then closed the door.

...

That evening the tavern at the inn was in full swing, with the piano ablaze and the bar full. All of the tables were in use, with a few poker games ongoing. Cole ordered food and went up to his room to eat with Tusk. He had ordered a full steak for the dog, who had not eaten since the attack. He cut a piece of meat and held it out for Tusk, who sniffed briefly and then ate it hungrily. It was a good sign. By the third piece of meat, he lifted his head and looked, as if to check how much more was available.

Cole lay down on the floor of the room after Tusk had eaten his fill. He mused at what people would think of a dog in a bed, while he rested on wooden planks, but this dog had saved his life and deserved any sacrifice he could make from now on, big or small.

Cole woke on the wood floor of the room, with light streaming in from the lone window. He had slept later than any time in memory. Tusk lay on the bed. Seeing Cole rise, the dog rotated to sit up more, whined with pain, but made it upright anyway. Cole smiled, with wet eyes. "We are going to make it back together, boy." He picked up his rucksack and left Tusk to rest in the room.

The town was active. There obviously had been more than one gold strike as the evidence of prosperity was in the full saloons and supply stores. New prospectors, fresh and eager, walked with a confident stride through town. Cole strolled through the active street and smiled, giving hellos to every passerby who smiled back. Last night, before falling asleep, he thought, *I've cheated death, every day now is a gift.*

He arrived at the refinery and nodded to the guards as he walked briskly inside.

"Well, if it isn't young Cole." Tom wore a broad smile and looked a tad proud even. "You said you would do it, and I believed you," he said excitedly. "It's a high quality too. Pure gold, as pure as we've had. Would you like to know how much?"

Cole nodded, and said with a wry smile, "It had occurred to me to ask."

"Two and a half pounds. That's over eight hundred dollars!" He looked expectantly at Cole, who flushed red and just shook his head.

"That's more than I needed, but we'll use it well."

Tom frowned a little at him and turned his head to one side, giving him an inquisitive look. "You're not done though. Wherever this rock was, it was part of a strain. There's almost sure to be a bunch more." Seeing no reaction from Cole, he added, "You have to go to the deeds office and stake a claim on the find."

Cole smiled softer now, looking thoughtful. "It's not on my way to where I'm going though, Tom."

"Not on the w … What?" Tom's voice was shrill in his exasperation. "There could be tens of thousands of dollars in gold out there where that rock was. Maybe more."

Cole shrugged. "You can go claim it. I'll draw you a map."

Tom stared at Cole, at first assuming it was a joke, but saw Cole's level gaze coming back at him. "I couldn't take that from you, it wouldn't be right?"

Cole placed his hands along the high desk. "You decide. I will take my money for the gold I gave you though."

Tom walked to the safe in the back of the room, shaking his head, then spun the dials one way and the other. With a loud click the door unlocked and he withdrew a bag with money in it. "I prepared this for you already, as the coach came yesterday, and I held enough cash for you but thought it'd be the first of many." He paused and thought for a moment. "I could pay you for a map to your claim if you're really not going back there. It wouldn't be much compared to what might be there cuz I haven't seen it. I could be buying a fortune, or nothing at all."

"Ok, Tom," Cole replied with a patient smile on his face.

"I can give you two hundred but I'm robbin' you blind, you know. Doesn't feel right," Tom said, still shaking his head.

"Well, I offered it to you for free, so you aren't very good at robbery if you're paying me two hundred dollars."

Tom retrieved the extra cash and handed it to Cole, who put the money in his sack and then wrote out directions to the location where he found the gold, as well as a crude map.

Handing the papers to Tom, he said, "You may find a couple of claim-jumpers nearby—but they won't cause any more trouble now."

As Tom took the papers, he grasped Cole's hand, looked into his eyes and said, "You're the strangest gold prospector I ever saw, boy. But I wish you luck where you're goin'."

...

Leaving the refinery, Cole felt at peace. He didn't care if there was more gold where he found it, in fact, he was almost certain there was, and he hoped Tom would find it. He had what he came for and needed to head home. He had several stops to make on his way back to the inn, though. He had business to finish in town before he left for home.

His first stop was the mission. The old man with the bent back greeted him kindly again. It was no surprise to Cole when he was told that Phoebe and her children were out somewhere in the northern territory doing mission work. Cole handed him twenty-five dollars and said, "Please take this donation to your mission and tell Phoebe it is in honor of Cyrus."

The next stop was to the brothel. The front porch had only one woman out, given the early hour of the day. Cole called out, "Good morning, I'm looking for Penny."

"I bet you are," the woman said with a knowing grin. He decided to let her make the lewd assumption and did not correct her. She leaned in the front door and yelled Penny's name, and a few moments later she emerged.

Cole waved for her to join him on the side of the building.

As they turned into the alley, he recalled that this was a place where he had seen men fucking women, and he briefly worried she would assume he had that intention, so he spoke quickly. "You were kind to me, and to my dog. I think you have as much skill as any doctor I've seen." He paused, reaching into his sack. "I came with your pay." He handed her twenty dollars, adding, "I can never repay the value of what you did for us."

Her eyes bulged and she started to speak but just stammered. Cole held up his hands and said, "Just don't tell anyone. I trust you. I'm headed home now and don't need anyone checking after me, if you know what I mean." Penny nodded, looking dazed, then put her arms around him and kissed his right cheek again.

...

Shopping at the general store felt different to Cole, knowing he could afford anything he needed for the trip home. He still would not be wasteful, but he wanted to have all he needed for a safe, fast journey home. He stocked up on beef jerky, which was easy to carry, would not go bad, and could nourish him along the way. He vowed not to eat fish for the entire trip, perhaps never again as long as he lived. He was grateful that the vast supply of river trout sustained them, but the thought of it now was nauseating.

He added potatoes and carrots, that would last the first week or so, and new clothes to replace his tattered, ragged jeans and shirts. He added a jacket for the coming colder months and a new burlap tent cover, to replace the one he had cut in two.

He spent almost five dollars but felt ready for the trip with one stop left.

The final stop required a trip to the stable. He gathered Little Boy and brought him to the tanners to fit for a saddle. This would be his biggest expense, perhaps even twenty-five dollars. The tanner was a burly man with a thick, dark mustache that curled up at the ends. He wore a leather apron and expensive-looking brown leather boots, befitting his trade. He looked at Cole and then Little Boy and toyed with the ends of his mustache. "That's a small mount but looks sturdy enough."

"He's been traveling with me for nearly a year—he's plenty sturdy." Cole gave the horse a pat on the head.

"I've got some smaller saddles, should fit his gullet well." He walked to the back of his shop and emerged with two small saddles. He placed the first one on Little Boy and then took out a narrow stick, whittled smooth, and pushed it under the saddle, checking for space. He then removed the saddle and repeated the measurement with the second one. "The first one fit better—if you like the look of it, we'll get it fit and buckled."

"It looks good on him. Thank you. How much?"

"Well, a bit less leather for the smaller saddle, but same work to make it. I can go twenty-two dollars."

"Let's make it twenty dollars even." Cole presumptively pulled the money out and handed it to the tanner, who did not protest.

"I'd like to buy some leather belts as well, wide and long." The tanner looked at Cole's narrow frame with a questioning look but sold him his three longest belts anyway.

…

Opening the door to his room at the inn, Cole was surprised to see Tusk standing on the bed, wagging his tail. He walked to the edge of the bed and looked down at the floor as if it were a leap of fifty feet, then looked back at Cole. He could not have asked for help more clearly if he had opened his mouth and spoken.

"Well, you're on your feet at least," Cole said, smiling at his dog. "I'll bet in a few days you'll be chasing bears again." Cole gently lifted the dog, eliciting a whimper, and placed him on the floor. Tusk took steps gingerly but walked on his own, looking up occasionally and wagging.

The innkeeper was paid, and the supplies were loaded on Little Boy. Cole spoke to his dog. "It'll be a few days at least before you can walk on your own, so let's see if this'll work." He applied more of the cleansing liquid to Tusk's stitched wound, then wrapped him in his old, tattered shirt and fastened the three leather belts loosely around the dog: one in a loop around his body just in front of his hind legs, another around his body just behind his front legs, and the last one between those. He then ran a length of rope through three loose belts above Tusk's back and lifted him. Hearing only a slight whimper, Cole felt it was bearable and would do no more damage. He ran the top end of the rope around the pommel of the saddle and hoisted the dog up the horse's left side, leaving Tusk's wound facing out.

Tusk weighed perhaps thirty-five pounds, Cole thought, and the supplies on the other side would counterbalance most of that. Plus, he hoped this would only be necessary for a few days. Tusk was resilient and showing signs of improving quickly.

The travelers were off on the long road home. Cole took one look back at the bustling town of Salem behind him. He wasn't sure if he would miss this place, but he would certainly remember it for the rest of his life.

As they found the path south of town, Cole saw a young prospector approaching on the trail. He looked to be a similar age to himself, but he looked so fresh and young compared to how Cole felt now. His stride was brisk, and he wore a hopeful smile, walking ahead of a pack mule that bore all the tools for exploration, including a gold pan hanging to one side.

As they passed one another, Cole nodded and said, "Good luck to you."

The young man grinned and replied, "Did ya find gold?"

"No, but plenty of others did, so there's hope."

December 1851 – Cold Spring, New York

There was a light dusting of early-season snow on the ground in the Hudson Valley. It made everything look fresh and new. Cole felt anything but fresh and new. His journey had aged him, but it was at an end now and he was about to be reunited with Belinda. Tears formed in his eyes as the town center of Cold Spring came into view. He looked down at Tusk, trotting by his side, and back at Little Boy, lagging behind, led by his tether. "We made it, boys. We're home."

The journey home had not been without challenges, but here they were. It had taken only two days of travel, back in the Oregon Territory, before Tusk refused to be strapped to the horse and demanded to walk on his own. He was slow at first, but within a week he seemed to be his old self. Cole thought about Penny and what a fine job she had done, a young girl in a brothel, doing the work of a doctor.

They had joined up for a while with a small group of prospectors headed back east. None had found gold, and they were all eventually beaten down by the monotony and disappointment inherent in the search. Cole went along with their stories and told his own about the days and nights of work with nothing but empty gold pans to show for it. He left out only the final week when he had found flecks that led to a large gold rock, and likely to a strain of gold that others would mine. To his fellow travelers, he was another beaten soul headed home with only wear and tear to show for his efforts.

He told them he'd gotten his nasty cut on the head from a fight over a poker game, which he decided was not actually a lie. The group had met along the road in the southeast of Oregon Territory and traveled together all the way to Independence, Missouri before each going their own ways. Cole was appreciative of the company, and the safety it brought. He had been so long on his own that any companionship was welcome.

He traveled mostly alone between Independence and Pittsburgh but occasionally joined with a family on their way back east. In Pittsburgh, he stayed again at the Old Stone Tavern. He saw the girl who had said, "You can call me Missy" and had guided him away from a card game with cheats.

"Hello, Priscilla," Cole said with a wry smile as she approached him, like a potential new customer. She looked surprised and stopped to study his face.

"You've got a girl, right?" She replied, recalling their conversation almost a year prior.

Now it was Cole's turn to look surprised. He handed her five dollars, put a finger to his mouth and said, "Our secret."

Most of the memories Cole reflected back on were of people who had treated him well, and he hoped that they recalled him similarly. Now, as he stood, staring at the pure beauty of Cold Spring, coated in white, he wondered if he would ever travel again, or if he would ever want to.

As he walked through town, he looked at the general store's front porch where Joseph Mills had held court and amazed the locals with his tales from the west and of finding gold. Cole resolved not to follow suit. His stories would be for his family only, perhaps with the exception of Joseph himself. He would need to give him the new gold pan as a replacement and buy him a new pickaxe.

He approached the Thomas and Wright family farms and decided he needed to go first to the Wright farm, which was where Belinda was more likely to be. He was excited and anxious but also nervous about seeing her again after so long. Would she see him the same way? He felt older; more worn. He even felt like a different person. What if he wasn't who she had loved so deeply anymore? He had always envisioned running the last mile to get to her, but he was walking slowly now, with trepidation.

Circling around the Thomas farm, he walked through a path that led to the Wright's farmhouse. He had to be sure his mother didn't see him yet, so as not to hurt her feelings by walking past. With dusk cascading a gray darkness around him, he was likely to be concealed. He stopped about one hundred yards from the Wright farmhouse. It was deadly silent and felt strange. Based on his stick mark counts, Cole felt sure it was Friday and the family should be here. There was no sound and no movement. He walked closer and saw that the front door had been boarded over. He stepped up cautiously and called out, "Blue, you home?" There was no response.

He pulled at the door and saw that new outer boards covered a hacked and mangled door behind it. It was obvious that someone had used an axe on the front door and Cole's heart pounded in his chest as he whispered to himself, "Tommy … no."

He wheeled around looking for anyone or anything suggesting what had happened here. He saw nothing and no one. He had been gone so long and it was all to save this farm. He wondered if he had been a fool. Then his eyes landed on the wooded thicket between the properties. This was where he met Belinda, more than seven years ago, where they had buried secrets together. He walked over to the hallowed ground beneath the trees. The snow coated the evergreens so perfectly it looked as if someone had painstakingly painted the top of each branch white. The ground underneath was bare, as the snowflakes had collected in the branches above like a tent cover.

Cole looked over the small mounds, each representing some hurt; some loss; some embarrassment he or Belinda had borne. Beyond these small mounds was something new, a large section of mounded ground that Cole was certain was not there when he left. It chilled him, but he did not know why. Tusk ran to the mound and began to dig furiously, making a hole quickly in the large mound of soil. Cole went to him and pulled him back.

Looking down, he noticed the dirt was somewhat loose. It had been placed here within the past year for sure. The hole that Tusk had started was already almost a foot deep, as the soil was easily moved, and despite the early season snow that had fallen in the Hudson Valley, the ground was not yet frozen. He dropped to his knees and put his hands into the hole and slowly pulled dirt out. A larger secret was buried here, and he wondered whether he should be looking, but he felt a strong pull. This mound meant something, and it might explain where the Wrights had gone; where Belinda had gone.

A few inches deeper than Tusk had dug, Cole's hand felt something that was neither dirt, nor root, nor rock. It gave way slightly as he brushed it. He cleared more dirt from its surface and saw it was leathery skin. He rocked backward, startled, and fell to his backside. Tusk pulled to get to the hole, but Cole held him back. After several minutes of racing thoughts and fears, he decided he had to unearth this secret.

Clearing more dirt, Cole could see gaps in the skin, decomposed and revealing dirt-filled, rotted flesh. Based on the size, it appeared to be a woman's lower leg. Cole's heart sank and fear and sadness gripped him as he began to see it as Belinda. He felt disgust with himself as he instinctively wished it would be her mother, or even Alice. Tears filled his eyes, and he began to uncover more of the limb, wanting to take the body out of the ground and see for himself, no matter the state of decay.

He worked his way down the leg to extract the foot but instead saw a bony hand. It wore a gold ring, with a cross. Tommy's ring. What he had seen as a woman's leg was the massive man's arm. The floodgates opened and Cole wept, collapsing backward and looking up through the trees, letting out loud sobs of joy and relief.

Cole sat up, wiping his tear-streaked face, and then rose to walk the short distance to his mother's house. Before leaving, he paused, then reached deep into his rucksack, which was tied amongst the various supplies on Little Boy's back. He walked slowly back to the hole that revealed Tommy's arm and placed a bear's tooth, tied to a leather rope, and a finely made Jim Bowie knife into Tommy's bony hand and closed it. Then he covered the hole and pressed down to pack it firmly.

...

Crossing the harvested fields, he saw his home, where he, Ma, and Dale lived so many happy years, rise up out of the ground in the distance, as he ascended the gentle slope of the fields. After a few more strides, the full farmhouse was revealed and his heart warmed. He smiled and thought of the people he hoped were inside. He could see lamplight through the windows and knew his reunion was near but was unsure with whom that reunion would be yet. He tied Little Boy to the railing above the broken newel post that Tommy had kicked in anger—it seemed like a different lifetime.

Standing on the porch, he heard conversation and laughter. There was a gathering inside. Cole thought, *It's Sunday dinner,* realizing he must have missed some notches in his stick. He was overwhelmed by the idea he would see his family, and hopefully Belinda, in a moment. He hesitated to open the door, in part wanting to relish this moment and in part for fear she would not be there. Tusk let out a bark and gave him away. All conversation inside stopped and there was total silence. He opened the door and the dog rushed in to screams of joy. The whole family ran to the hall and stared toward the door, frozen for a moment; Ma, Dale, Katherine, all of the Wrights, and Belinda, pushing between them all to stand in front, her brilliant blue eyes wet with tears.

They rushed to each other and held each other so hard that neither could breathe. The family crushed around them in a circle so tight it seemed impossible to include nine people, plus a dog.

...

That night they ate, drank, and talked until the morning hours. Alice and Buck went into Cole's bedroom with Tusk and fell asleep near midnight and Eleanor woke up, needing attention from her parents. At about a year and a half, she looked like a small version of Dale, who remained as proud today as the day she was born. Cole shared stories of his journey west and of the Oregon Territory. He left out anything about pain or struggles, but his scarred forehead and Tusk's disfigured left side revealed that there were parts of the story missing—parts they knew not to ask about, at least not yet. Dale laughed at hearing about the poker game, telling Katherine, "I lost every time to him as kids."

Ma and Belinda sat on either side of Cole, pulling stools so close they were pressing into each of his sides. When he told them all about the day he found gold, after detailing his level of despair that he might never find it, they whooped and clapped. He told them about Tom at the refinery and how he'd paid extra for the claim, sight unseen, but that good man still felt he was robbing Cole.

Katherine yawned tiredly, holding Eleanore, who was again asleep, draped over her mother with arms and legs dangling over the side of the rocker. Dale stood and said, "We'd best be going," then looked at Cole, smiled, and said, "I'm glad you're back."

It was short but heartfelt, and Cole knew his brother had missed him. He realized at that moment how much he had missed his brother, though it had been overshadowed by the massive weight of longing for Belinda.

Dale and his family shuffled out, exhausted but happy. Ma turned to Maye Wright and nodded toward the bedroom where Alice and Buck had gone to sleep. "With the young ones down, you might as well stay and take them home in the morning. Cole and Belinda can go back and make sure all's right at your farm."

Mrs. Wright looked puzzled for a moment, thinking about the odd suggestion to stay here when her farm was right next door, then recognition swept across her face. "Oh, yes. Why don't you kids go on and we'll be back in the morning—perhaps after breakfast, if you'll have us to eat here, Elizabeth."

"Of course. We'll have a nice breakfast here and you'll head home with the young ones midmorning." The women smiled at each other.

The whole setup was so painfully obvious that Cole and Belinda shook their heads and smiled, but they were too eager to be alone to care. They said good night and walked outside. Ma followed and caught Cole on the front steps. He had stepped down one stair when she turned him around, so they now stood eye-to-eye. She looked at his forehead with the angry scar and tipped her head up to kiss it, then pulled him close and held her son. "I never knew I could miss anyone like this." She wiped tears away and said, "Now git. I'll see you tomorrow." And she walked briskly back in, leaving him no time to respond.

Cole and Belinda walked slowly, hand-in-hand, toward the Wright farm. He looked over at her every few steps as if making sure she was real, not a dream. "You know, I was talking all night about my adventure, but I haven't heard about yours. It's quite a thing to have kept that farm going with only an old woman and two kids to help you."

"There's time for that. Your family needed to hear about your time." She paused, "And we didn't hear all of it yet, did we?"

"There's time for that too," he said with a smile.

As they reached the fence, they stepped through, and both looked under the trees at the mounds of secrets. Cole looked at the large, new mound and said, "You've had to bury more secrets." He touched her face and kissed her lips softly.

Belinda looked down at the mound. Her mind flashed back to the moment she thought her life was over. She raised the rifle with her left and steadied it. Her right hand, freshly broken, moved to the trigger but simply would not work. She lowered the gun and looked up, seeing Tommy, in all of his rage, striped with thin beams of pale moonlight through the planks. He raised the axe, it glinted and began to come down, then she heard a shrill cry and the tines of a pitchfork shot out the front of Tommy's neck. A stripe of light showed the shock in his eyes as the axe fell from his hands. He dropped to his knees and fell face first to the barn floor, the pitchfork handle now vertical, blood flowing from his neck, forming a red pool around his head. Maye Wright stood shaking in the darkness behind her fallen son.

Belinda held her gaze on the mound, stepped back from Cole, rubbed her now-healed right hand, and said, "I hope you don't mind, but I let Mama in on our place. She had a secret to bury too."

Understanding crept over Cole's face slowly and he nodded. "I buried a few secrets of my own here tonight." He paused, adding, "but I suspect we won't be needing to do that again."

"I hope you're right," she replied and took his hand as they walked into the farmhouse, through the roughly repaired door. She led Cole to her bed and pulled off his shirt, then knelt down to unbutton his jeans. He slid them down and stepped out of them and stood naked as he undressed her. They lay down, silently looking at each other in near darkness, seeing only curves and shadows. He gently slid his hand down her breast and rubbed it lightly and she reached between his legs and guided him inside her.

They moved together, slowly, kissing each other as they had years before, their lips holding one another's. They seemed to breathe in unison as they moved. In minutes they both succumbed to the pleasure and gasped. As it ended, they lay there still, neither wanting to move, nor to stop being joined together. They had spent so much time apart, now they wanted to stay like this forever.

An hour passed and they had not moved apart, Cole was still inside her and he came to life again. They began to move together as if they had never stopped and this time the sensation was even stronger. They lay there again for a long time after. Cole rolled to his back with Belinda's head on his shoulder. She ran her fingers over his chest and said, "So, I guess we aren't waiting 'til we're married."

She could feel his smile in the darkness as he said, "We've been married since the day we met, in every way that really matters."

Epilogue:

May 1914 – Cold Spring, New York

*T*he walk into the center of Cold Spring from the farm took longer these days. Belinda and Cole strolled slowly; her left hand interlaced with his right. They made this walk, which was now on paved roads, once per week in the warmer months. Today was a glorious day in the Hudson Valley, with a warm sun and a gentle breeze. When they looked at the trees, and not down at the paved road, this could as well have been 1846 as 1914. Cole kicked a rock that sat on top of the paved surface past Belinda's legs, and she looked at him, with her head tilted and shaking side-to-side a little to indicate she was not going to play this game. He chuckled.

It had been more than sixty-two years since they spoke their vows officially, but they both regarded this year as their seventieth anniversary. In all the years since Cole returned from the West, they had never spent a day apart and that suited them both well.

Belinda stood straight and looked younger than her eighty-one years. Her silver hair still flowed down to her shoulders.

Her face had become creased with lines worthy of her age. She was slim and her eyes were as blue as the day they had met. Cole had a slight stoop at his shoulders but remained fairly agile and slim. His hair had thinned and turned pure white. He still wore a smile most of the time, with deep smile lines visible on his face.

On these walks, they no longer sought out which buildings or roads were new, but rather focused on what was unchanged since the walks in their youth. A surprising number of buildings near the center of town remained mostly unchanged, including the general store, which was now a pharmacy.

The Thomas and Wright farms had been combined five years earlier when Katherine died a year after Dale had passed. None of their four children wanted the farm, so Belinda and Cole bought it from their children and removed the fence that ran along the border. In all practical manners, the farms had run together for decades, with the two families helping each other and deciding on crop rotations together.

Four generations of their family now lived on the combined farm. Belinda gave birth to two children within the first two years after Cole returned. The first was born nine months after he got back and they liked to think he was conceived on their first night together, but in truth, they had made love so many times those first weeks, there was no way to know. They named the baby Cyrus to honor the man Cole buried on his way to the Oregon Territory, or perhaps more so to honor his wife, Phoebe, who endured a perilous road with Cole that neither may have survived alone. When Wyoming achieved statehood in 1890,

Cole had looked over maps and figured that Cyrus was buried somewhere in that state.

About fourteen months after Cyrus came Elizabeth-Maye. Belinda had insisted on naming their first girl after the two women who had saved her life. Their third child, Isabelle, never drew a living breath, and Belinda was so brokenhearted that she never wanted to conceive again.

Isabelle's small grave lay in the family plot that had grown through the years. Maye Wright passed in her late forties from a wasting disease. Elizabeth Thomas died at seventy-six, peacefully in her sleep. Dale and Katherine joined the plot half a decade ago and Alice just last year. Buck was still alive and well, living in Albany, but it had started to feel like almost everyone they had known in their youth had passed on. One of the earliest markers on the family plot was for Tusk, the only one of their many dogs through the years that was buried with the family. Tusk lived another six years after their adventure and thus got to be part of the children's early lives. At every visit to the family plot, Cole would lay a hand on the small stone that marked his grave and thank the dog who had brought him to Belinda, had saved his life, and been a dear friend.

The "children" as Cole liked to call them still, with a wry smile, because they were in their early sixties, each had three children of their own. The six grandchildren ranged from twenty-eight to forty-three now, and their offspring, the great-grand-children, numbered thirteen in total, so far. All-in-all, seven of their descendants, plus three spouses lived on the farm which now had two additional small homes on it. The rest had taken on other careers, but all visited regularly.

Upon returning from their weekly walk to town, one of their grandsons asked Belinda and Cole if he could clear the thicket of trees between the old border of the Thomas and Wright farms. The fence had been gone for years and the trees took up valuable land that could be farmed. They asked him to leave that space as it was and then walked out to the thicket, hand-in-hand, to look over the ground. The contour had softened over the decades, and it was hard to tell where different secrets were buried. No one had ever come looking for Tommy, nor for Lev or Burl. The bones, the bear-tooth necklace, and the Bowie knife had been buried shallow in the ground between their farms, but deep enough to have held their secrets.

Afterword

Even a month before I began writing Cold Spring, I would not have believed this story was about to pour out. While I have written in short form all my life, a novel was not in my plans until suddenly it was. The kernel of a story came to mind one day and gnawed at me until I decided to start writing it down. I quickly became obsessed with telling the full tale and thought of little else until it was complete.

The broad story arc was in my head but the details came into view as words filled the pages. At times I felt like I was reading the book as much as writing it. I love historical fiction and have always been fascinated by how people lived before all of the trappings of modern convenience we enjoy today. Writing this story led me to delve into research about life on a northern farm in the mid-nineteenth century, as well as the Gold Rush and Oregon Trail.

It was an experience I'll treasure and I hope you have enjoyed reading Cold Spring.

Glenn Shapiro is a lifelong writer of poetry and short stories. Cold Spring is his first novel at the start of his "second act" after retirement. Born and raised in the Northeast of the United States, he has always been fascinated by colonial times and poured that curiosity and research into his first novel.